Mended Hearts

TARA CONRAD

HIS ONE HER ONLY PUBLISHING

Contents

Dear Readers — v

Svetlana — 1
Brandon — 4
Svetlana — 8
Svetlana — 12
Svetlana — 20
Brandon — 23
Svetlana — 31
Svetlana — 37
Brandon — 42
Svetlana — 49
Svetlana — 57
Brandon — 61
Svetlana — 65
Svetlana — 72
Svetlana — 76
Brandon — 79
Brandon — 82
Svetlana — 85
Brandon — 89
Svetlana — 93
Brandon — 100
Brandon — 106
Svetlana — 111
Svetlana — 113
Svetlana — 119
Brandon — 124
Svetlana — 128
Slava — 133
Svetlana — 140
Svetlana — 145

Svetlana   151
Brandon   158
Svetlana   163
Brandon   171
Svetlana   175
Brandon   180
Svetlana   186
Brandon   191
Svetlana   198
Brandon   203
Svetlana   211

Also by Tara Conrad   214
About Tara   215
Acknowledgments   216
Resources   217

Dear Readers

I'd like to offer a gentle and thoughtful heads-up before you embark on the journey within the pages of this book. Within its storyline, you will encounter themes that revolve around the deeply sensitive and personal topics of pregnancy loss and infertility.

While using my personal experience with this topic, I've done my best to ensure the themes are handled with utmost care and respect, aiming to portray the emotional complexities that individuals and couples may experience. It's my intention to provide a realistic and empathetic portrayal, shedding light on the struggles and resilience of those who face such challenges. However, I understand these topics can evoke strong feelings, memories, and personal experiences for many readers.

If you find that these themes hit too close to home or may trigger difficult emotions, I urge you to consider your emotional well-being before proceeding. Should you decide to continue reading, I encourage you to reach out for support if needed. Remember that you are not alone, and seeking help from friends, family, or professionals is always a valid option.

My hope is that this fiction story provides a window into the lives of its characters, fostering insight, understanding, and a profound sense of connection for those who've experienced similar journeys, as well as for those who seek to empathize with these experiences. I wish to extend my deepest appreciation for your willingness and openness in exploring these themes with my characters and me.

With empathy and respect,

~Tara

Svetlana

✍

Pregnant.

I'm pregnant.

When everyone left for New York to welcome Alex and Natalie home, I was sure I had the flu and wasn't up to traveling. Brandon and I stayed in Russia so I could recover. Our visit became extended when *Dandekar* Konstantin, Mama's older brother, surprised us with a visit.

Konstantin is a high-ranking general in the Russian army and is stationed in Novosibirsk. The Russian military is the opposite of most other countries in that the higher your rank, the less leave you get. We hadn't seen him in several years, and I was excited to introduce him to Brandon and spend time visiting with him.

I thought my period was late because of all the stress I'd been under. Knowing my pregnant best friend and her husband were abducted by one of the most notorious traffickers in the world was a living, breathing nightmare. But my doctor's visit earlier today and the ultrasound picture I now hold say otherwise.

Although Brandon and I have been back in New York for almost two weeks, I've only spoken to Natalie on video chat. I wanted to tell her about Brandon's proposal and my newest secret, but she and Alex have literally been to hell and back the

"

past month. She was malnourished and had some complications that kept her on bed rest for a few weeks. I wanted to visit her, but Alex insisted on no visitors while they healed both mentally and physically. Thankfully, she and the baby survived their harrowing ordeal and have made a full recovery.

Standing in front of my mirror, I pull up my shirt and place my hands on my still-flat stomach. "Hi, *kroshechnaya babochka,*" I say to my unborn child—my tiny butterfly. "I can't wait to tell your daddy about you. He's going to be so happy."

I tuck the ultrasound photo in the hidden pocket of my purse and go into the bathroom for a quick shower. Alex planned a surprise collaring ceremony for Natalie tonight. Something that's become quite the habit with him. Natalie's none the wiser and thinks it's a farewell dinner for my parents. I can't wait to see the look on her face when she realizes what's actually happening. After everything they've endured, they deserve happiness.

As much as I believe that to be true, I'm still struggling with jealousy. I want to be celebrating our engagement and pregnancy. Instead, I'm sitting on the sidelines, watching and waiting. After I put my clothes in the laundry basket, I step into the shower. With my eyes closed, I stand under the stream of hot water, using it to wash away the unwanted envy.

Arms wrap around my waist, and I scream.

"It's just me," Brandon says, laughing.

"You scared the shit out of me." I turn around and slap his chest.

"I'm sorry," he says with a mischievous grin. Pulling me against him, he leans down to kiss me. "When I saw you naked, I couldn't help myself."

The way Brandon looks at me, a mix of desire and tenderness in his gaze, sends a shiver of anticipation down my spine. Brandon traces my jawline with his thumb, causing my heart to skip a beat. His hands slide lower until they cup my ass. He lifts me, and I wrap my legs around his waist as he kisses me. The sensation of water droplets caressing my skin, combined with my heightened arousal, is exhilarating.

This feels so different. Brandon's taking his time as though he's savoring the intimacy of the moment. With my back against the smooth tile of the shower, he slides his hard length inside me. With every touch, every gentle stroke, he's exploring my contours as though it's our first time. Brandon's worshipping of my body extends beyond purely physical, as though he's deepening an emotional and spiritual connection between us.

I love the feel of his muscles flexing beneath my hands as he moves his body with fluid motions alternating between teasing my opening with the tip of his cock and thrusting deeply. The circling of his hips creates beautiful friction against my clitoris.

"You're so tight," Brandon says between kisses. "It feels so good."

"Mhm."

We're entwined in an intimate dance. The mingling of our breaths creates a symphony of desire. We move in harmony as we build toward a shared crescendo. I cry out as pleasure explodes in rippling waves. Brandon follows me as we float freely through the melody of euphoria.

He puts his forehead against mine as the water flows over us, washing away everything, leaving only the profound connection we share. Time stands still as we hold tightly to each other, savoring the moment of being lost in one another.

Brandon

SVETLANA LOOKS REGAL IN HER FLOWING WHITE DRESS that shimmers beneath the glow of the twinkling lights. Right now, she's talking with Star's current submissive, Zayne. The two are laughing and having a good time. As though she senses me watching her, Lana looks over her shoulder. A radiant smile spreads across her face.

The buzzing of the phone in my pocket steals my attention.

Alex: We're pulling up now.

Me: Thanks for the heads up. We're ready for you.

"Excuse me," I call, and everyone turns my way. "They're pulling up now. Please take your places, and then we'll turn the lights off."

There's a hushed murmur as the Dominants take their places around the edge of the circular garden. The submissives, all dressed in white, kneel before their Dominants. After Maxim and Irina arrive and take their place, they'll complete the circle surrounding Alex as he collars Natalie.

The clang and groan of the tall gate opening fill the darkness.

"Are you ready?" Alex asks.

"Ready for what?" The words barely leave Natalie's mouth

when the lights turn on. "What's going on, Sir?" she asks, looking around in disbelief.

"No more talking, baby girl." Alex steps away from her to stand in the center of the circle.

Maxim takes his place next to me as Irina gracefully kneels at his feet.

"Natalie, please join your Dominant," I instruct.

Lana reaches out and grabs Natalie's hand as she walks by. The girls exchange a smile.

Alex motions toward a black silk blanket laid on the ground in front of him. "Kneel." He holds Natalie's hand to steady her as she takes her place. "Look at me."

I walk to the center, stand beside Alex, and hand him the velvet box containing Natalie's collar. Alex removes the lid and angles it to show Natalie. Her breath catches when she sees the silver chain with the heart-shaped lock next to it.

Alex clears his throat before he addresses his guests. "I'm thankful for each of you who came tonight to share this special evening with us. The last few weeks have been the scariest of my life. Not only was I unsure if I'd live to see another day, but my submissive, the most precious person in my life, was in grave danger. Even though we're back safely, we're both still healing." His voice cracks, and he struggles to maintain his composure. "I had this collar made before all that happened. Since we've been back, I've struggled with how to proceed. I wasn't sure if I should let more time pass before offering a collar to my submissive, fearing it would trigger her."

The Dominants and submissives gathered here tonight are our closest friends. They know Maxim works to stop human trafficking, but they don't know the full extent of what he does or how deeply Alex and I are involved. However, they all know about Alex and Natalie's abduction—how close we all came to losing them.

"I sought the advice of a wise friend." He looks toward Star, and the corners of his mouth turn up. "Who explained to me that the piece of leather Natalie was forced to wear was meaningless—it held no significance in our lifestyle or relationship. This collar in my hand is the one that holds meaning and commitment, the only one that matters. I decided to take a chance and seize the moment because no one is guaranteed a tomorrow. I didn't want to let another day go by without my submissive knowing how much I treasure her. How much it will mean to me if she accepts my collar."

Alex lifts the collar and hands me the empty box. I clasp his shoulder before returning to my place in front of Svetlana.

"Natalie, as your Dominant, your heart, your safety, your life are mine to care for. I'm honored that you've chosen to submit to me. I cherish that submission. Tonight, I'm asking you to take your commitment to us one step further. I'm asking you to wear my collar." He stops to clear his throat. "By accepting this collar, you demonstrate your commitment to our relationship and your willingness to submit to me both physically and emotionally. You promise to obey me and accept my guidance, knowing I will care for and protect you in every way. Moreover, this collar represents my commitment to continue to train and support you, always respecting your boundaries and helping you grow in your submission. Above all, I promise to cherish and protect you for as long as we live. So, Natalie, I ask you now. Will you accept this collar and all the promises it symbolizes?"

"Yes, Sir. I will," Natalie replies, her commitment evident in her words.

Natalie holds her hair up as Alex places the silver chain around her neck and attaches the lock. "Thank you for your gift of submission, baby girl."

As I look around the circle, I notice there isn't a dry eye. We've all been privileged to witness this intimate exchange as Alex and Natalie take their dynamic to the next level.

After the ceremony concludes, Anthony escorts us to a separate area that's set for a meal. Each couple has a private table where we enjoy a seven-course dinner. Lana's uncharacteristically quiet while we eat. "What's wrong?"

Lana's eyes widen. "What do you mean?"

"You haven't said two words since we sat down," I observe.

"I'm taking everything in." She scans the surroundings. "This is all a lot."

"Collaring is a serious step in any dynamic," I state, setting my fork down. "I'm hoping we take this step. Soon."

Lana takes a sip of her ice water. "That sounds wonderful."

"What is it you aren't saying?" I press gently.

"We have our engagement to announce," she whispers. "And you'd like to have a collaring. I don't want anyone to think we're copying whatever Alex and Natalie are doing."

"I get it, but I don't think anyone would feel that way," I remark skeptically.

"What if," she says thoughtfully. "When we get married, we have a dual ceremony?"

"I'm not sure I'm following," I admit, intrigued.

"A wedding and collaring. Something kinky and fun," Lana proposes with a mischievous smile.

"I like the way you think," I reply, a grin spreading across my face.

Svetlana

I MORE THAN LIKE THE IDEA. I LOVE THE IDEA OF NOT only becoming Brandon's wife but also being collared by him. As much as I loved the idea of a Dom/sub dynamic, a part of me feared I'd feel trapped or voiceless. I dreamt of having a Dominant of my own, but at the same time, I couldn't see myself finding contentment or freedom. Until Brandon, I never fully understood how freeing submission truly is.

I finally understand what Masha said to me all those years ago. That when I found the right Dominant, my submission would be a gift I'd willingly give. She doesn't like this lifestyle, so I blew her off. I wish I could tell her how right she was and how wrong I was.

My life and heart are safe with Brandon. Gifting him my submission has been the best decision I've ever made. Brandon's my anchor amidst the tumultuous storms of life. He's my rock when I'm weak and ready to give up. Knowing I'm going to spend forever with him is a wonderful secret to have, but I'm aching to slip my engagement ring back on my finger and announce to the world that I said yes. Brandon keeps saying that Natalie and Alex won't be upset if we announce our engagement, too. I'm sure he's right, but I don't want to take any of the attention from them. It just doesn't seem right.

"Svetlana," Papa says and waves his hand in front of my face. "Yes?"

"What is on your mind, *moya babochka*?" He sits in the chair next to me.

"Nothing, really." I shrug.

"You were a million miles away."

"I guess I was daydreaming a bit." My gaze drifts across the courtyard to where Brandon and Owen are talking.

"That man is very much in love with you," Papa says softly. "I believe you will get your happily ever after one day very soon."

"Do you really think so?" I turn my attention to Papa.

"I do." He leans over and kisses my cheek. "We are getting ready to leave. Mama wants to say goodbye."

"I wish you could stay longer." My heart breaks a little each time they leave.

"Brandon will be flying out in a few weeks. You should come with him."

"I wish I could. The law firm I'm interning with is in the middle of a big criminal case. I can't leave right now."

"You'll be very proud of her, Max," Brandon says as he walks up next to me. "She was chosen over fifty other applicants."

"I have always known the potential that Svetlana has. It is about time the rest of the world also sees it." Papa beams with pride.

"Alright, you two." I push my chair out and get to my feet. "I'm going to say goodbye to Mama."

On the way inside the restaurant, Papa and Brandon get stopped by Alex. I leave them behind and go find her. Mama's standing off to the side, talking on her cell phone. She doesn't see me coming, which gives me a minute to watch her.

She's beginning to show signs of aging. Her dark hair is peppered with grey. I think it looks stunning, but Mama's unsure if she wants to color it or keep it natural. Fine lines extend from the corners of her eyes. We call them *linii kharaktera* or character lines. She's insecure about the physical changes that come with her age, but I think she's only growing more beautiful. Her head turns, and a smile spreads across her face. She holds a finger up, letting me know she's almost done with her phone call.

I nod and walk over to the windows overlooking the street, giving her privacy to finish her call. Outside, Misha stands against their black car. Although he's talking with Viktor and Pyotr, his eyes continually scan the area.

"I wish those boys would find a woman. Or a man," Mama adds.

"Pyotr and Viktor?" I ask, surprised.

Misha is married and has a few children, but Pyotr and Viktor are single. I've never considered Pyotr's personal life—or lack thereof. Something very selfish on my part. And Viktor, I honestly don't know how any woman could tolerate his overprotectiveness. I see how he is with Natalie, and they're not even in a relationship. I can only imagine how much worse he'd be if he were with someone.

"They've been loyal to our family for so long. I would love to see them find love. I have friends with single daughters," Mama says and sighs loudly. "But your papa doesn't want me meddling in their lives. Enough of that." She turns to me. "When will we see you again?"

"I'm not sure. My internship is taking up more time than I thought it would. And I have my bar exam scheduled for November."

"I can't believe my little girl is all grown up."

"There you are," Papa says as he walks toward us. "Are you ready to leave, *moya vozlyublenny*?"

"I'm never ready to say goodbye."

Papa wraps his arm around Mama. "We will see her again soon."

After we say our goodbyes, they leave the restaurant and get into the car. Tears run down my face as I watch them drive away.

"Hey," Brandon says, wiping the moisture from my cheeks. "Why are you crying?"

"It's been hard watching from the sidelines and wishing it was us."

"We don't have to wait. Alex and Natalie won't be mad if we announce our engagement."

"I know." I thread my fingers with Brandon's. "But it's important to let them have this time. I know we'll get our turn."

"We will, *mon petite papillon.*"

Svetlana

BRANDON: I NEED YOU IN THE OFFICE.

Me: Can I have ten minutes, Sir?

I'm in the middle of putting dinner together and need to get it into the oven if we're going to eat at a decent time.

Brandon: Put aside whatever you're doing and come up.

I roll my eyes but turn the burner off and set the pan aside. In a display of annoyance, I walk up the stairs, ensuring my footsteps are a little louder than they should be. When I get to the office doorway, I nearly collide with Brandon.

"Put this on," he says, handing me one of his T-shirts.

"You want me to get dressed?" I ask in confusion. Brandon prefers to keep me naked at home.

"Yes. Max and Irina are on video chat."

"Why?" In a panic, I hurry to pull the shirt over my head. "Is there something wrong?"

"They didn't say, but I don't think so." I follow Brandon to the desk and see my parents' images on the screen. "She's here," he says as he takes his seat.

"What's wrong?" I grab Brandon's hand, preparing myself for some unknown awful news.

"Hello to you, too." Papa laughs.

"Hi. What's wrong?"

"There is nothing wrong. Your Mama and I have news we want to share."

"Okay," I say hesitantly. Brandon tugs my hand gently, and I sit on his lap.

"You remember that young Australian girl Natalie met at Moreno's compound?" Mama asks.

"Amelia?"

"Yes, Amelia." Mama smiles warmly. "We promised Natalie we would personally oversee her treatment, so we brought her to Jelena's Hope."

My parents see Natalie as another daughter, so it doesn't surprise me that they made that promise. "How is she?"

"She's doing as well as to be expected," Irina states.

"Amelia is strong. She will do well," Papa adds.

"You've met her?"

Early in their recovery, most of the girls distrust men. Despite his kind and caring disposition, Papa's appearance is intimidating. For that reason, he typically doesn't interact with the girls until much later in their treatment.

"I have. Amelia is an exception." Papa and Mama exchange a smile. "We have decided to adopt her."

"Congratulations," Brandon says without missing a beat.

Certain I misheard, I ask, "Can you repeat that?"

"Amelia and I have been working closely at the center," Mama explains. "She's an exceptional young lady. We've bonded rather quickly."

"Your mama introduced us a few weeks ago, and although it has been a little rocky, we are slowly getting to know one another," Papa adds with a smile on his face. "Your Mama and I already love the girl and wish to legally adopt her."

My parents are the most loving and giving people I know. The fact that they're opening not only their home but their hearts to another child doesn't surprise me at all.

"We've talked to her therapist about how best to approach the subject and will ask Amelia very soon. We wanted to tell you before we brought it up to her. We weren't sure how you'd feel about it," Mama says hesitantly.

Excitement bubbles inside. I feel like a little kid on Christmas morning. "I'm going to have a little sister?"

"Yes, *moya babochka*." He takes Mama's hand in his. "Your mama and I hope you will be okay with this."

"Of course, I'm okay with it. I'm thrilled."

"Congratulations, big sis," Brandon says and kisses my cheek. "When do we get to meet her?"

"She's here now if you'd like to talk to her. Please don't bring up the adoption," Mama says.

"I won't." I bounce on Brandon's lap from sheer excitement. He grabs my hips, stilling me.

Mama leaves the view of the camera to get Amelia.

"How old is she?" I inquire.

"Fifteen," Papa replies, and a dark shadow crosses his face.

"The same age as Jelena," I mumble.

Papa lowers his voice. "Amelia is still very timid."

It isn't lost on me that he ignored my comment.

"She'll come around." Brandon tries to encourage him.

"Come on, sweetheart. It's okay." I hear Mama before I see her.

When Amelia comes into view, concern overtakes me, and I struggle to keep a smile on my face. She's tiny and so very thin— far too thin for her age. Her long red hair is dull and lifeless. Amelia's hazel eyes dart back and forth between Papa and Mama.

"Amelia," Papa says. "I would like to introduce you to our daughter, Svetlana, and her boyfriend, Brandon."

"Hello," she whispers.

"It's very nice to meet you," I say as cheerfully as possible. "I've heard a lot about you."

"You have?" she asks without looking up.

My heart aches. I feel her terror from here and can only imagine the hell she lived through at Moreno's hands.

"Will you ladies excuse me for a minute?" Papa stands, causing Amelia to startle. "I have to attend to something. I will be back in a few minutes."

"Natalie told me about you."

"You know Natalie?" She glances at the screen, her eyes wide.

"Brandon and I both do. Natalie's my best friend."

"Really?" The corners of her mouth turn up in a smile.

"Cross my heart." I grin.

"Mr. Max," she says, looking over her shoulder. "He said I'll get to talk to Natalie."

"I'm sure you will."

"Amelia has been a guest in our home the past two nights," Mama says. "She's staying in your room."

"Miss Irina said you wouldn't be mad." She wrings her hands. Her body is still on high alert. "I haven't touched any of your stuff."

"I'm not mad at all. And you're more than welcome to touch anything in there," I say, keeping my voice soft, hoping to ease her nerves. "There's a bunch of clothes in my closet. You can look through them and take anything you want."

"Really?"

"Really," I giggle.

"You were right," she whispers to Mama. "She's very nice."

"I'm glad you think so." Mama pats Amelia's hand.

"May I be excused now?" she asks cautiously.

"Sweetheart, you don't have to ask."

"I forgot. I'm sorry." Amelia turns back to me. "It was nice to meet you. If you talk to Natalie, can you please tell her I miss her?"

"I will. I promise."

Amelia gives a small wave before turning and leaving.

Mama waits until she's out of the room before speaking. "She's not comfortable around your papa."

"I see that."

"That's the thing that worries me most." Mama's eyebrows pinch together. "I'm hoping they can work through it."

The door cracks open, and Papa peeks in. "Is she gone already?"

"Amelia was having a snack with Olga when I got her. I think she wanted to finish." Mama turns back to me. "She and Olga get along very well."

"I am envious," Papa says as he sits. "The child is terrified of me."

"You're a good man, Max," Brandon says, leaning closer to the screen. "Once she sees that, she'll come around."

"I hope you are right."

"Are you sure it's still a good time for me to come out?" Brandon asks.

"That is one of the reasons I called. It is best if we hold off on your trip for a few weeks. We are hoping to have Amelia stay here a little longer. It is hard enough with my men and me. I do not want to scare her more than she already is."

"My schedule's wide open. When you're ready, let me know."

"I knew you would understand," Papa says, then turns his attention to me. "I hope you will consider coming with Brandon and meeting the child."

"I'll see what I can do."

"I will be in touch."

We say our goodbyes, and the screen goes black.

"How are you really feeling?" Brandon asks.

"I'm shocked. But I'm so happy." I shift on his lap so I can see him. "I can't believe I'm going to have a little sister."

"Your parents have so much to offer a child. Amelia's a lucky little girl."

I can't help but think Jelena had a hand in this. That somehow, she brought Amelia to our family.

"Now, about what you did to me by bouncing all over my lap like you did," Brandon says with a mischievous smile.

"Surely, I don't know what you mean." I bite my lower lip.

Brandon takes my hand and puts it over his hard cock. "Does this give you any hints?"

"Maybe."

With his hands on my hips, he removes me from his lap and pushes his chair back.

My hands go to his belt, undoing it, and then work on his button and zipper. He lifts his hips, allowing me to slide his pants and boxer briefs down his muscular legs. I lower to my knees between his spread thighs.

I run my thumb along the slit, already glistening with pre-cum, and then lean forward and do the same with my tongue. My lips feather kisses along the soft skin at the head of his dick, and my tongue makes gentle swirls. Without warning, I take him all the way in until he hits the back of my throat. Brandon takes a deep breath and drops his head back.

Taking my time, I worship his body with languid movements that alternate between shallow and deep. My hand plays with his balls while I suck and nip at him. His breathing turns shallower, and I know at any minute, he'll fuck my mouth roughly. It's a powerful game of cat and mouse, seeing how far I can push him before he loses control.

I let the tip slip out of my mouth and trail kisses down his length until I reach the base. Then I take him back in, allowing him to feel the tightness of my throat around his cock. He moans as I continue to lick and suck. Slowly, I move my hand up and down his shaft in time with my mouth. He lifts his hips up, encouraging me to give him more. I pull away and look up at him.

He's so sexy with his eyes closed and his chest rising and falling. Knowing it's me doing this to him is arousing. I consider sliding my hand through my wet folds and bringing myself to orgasm with him, but I stop myself and focus all my energy on Brandon.

Needing to taste him again, I let my tongue trace the ridges of his cock, and then I take him deeper. The tip hits the back of my throat again. I hold myself there for a moment and then slowly pull back. Brandon's had enough of my teasing. He grabs my hair and thrusts himself all the way into my mouth. His move catches me off guard, and I gag, but he doesn't let go.

"Relax and take my cock," he growls.

He fucks my face hard and fast. It takes all my concentration to relax my throat and take it all. Brandon pulls my head back and then lifts his hips, ensuring I take all of him. He swells even bigger, and I know he's close.

"Do you feel what you do to me?" he asks. I nod. "Do you like sucking my cock, *papillon*? Tell me you love sucking my cock."

He loosens his hold so I can answer him. "I love sucking your cock, Sir."

Those words make him lose all control. With both hands on my head, he slams his cock into my mouth.

"Fuck," he roars, and I moan against his dick.

I feel the first pulses of his orgasm hitting the back of my throat. I swallow everything he has to give me before licking him clean.

"You're going to be the death of me," he says as he pulls me from my knees so I straddle him, and he kisses me deeply. I rub my pussy back and forth on his still-hard dick. "I need to be inside you now."

I line him up with my opening and lower myself onto him. My head drops back, and I moan loudly.

"Fuck me," he commands, and I oblige, riding him hard and fast.

I grind my clit against him, driving myself closer to orgasm. Closing my eyes, I lose myself in the rhythm of our bodies. Brandon wraps his hands around my waist and pulls me up and down on his cock faster and harder. I scream out his name as my body squeezes his cock. He follows me over the edge, and I feel him explode inside me. My orgasm seems to go on forever as I milk every last drop of cum from him before I collapse onto his chest.

Wrapped in each other's embrace, the rest of the world fades away. It's only him and me. I wish we could stay in this moment forever.

Svetlana

ONE DAY FADES INTO THE NEXT UNTIL THEY'RE nothing but a jumbled blur. My mind is fuzzy. The information I'm studying feels like it's going through my head like a siphon. I can't seem to remember anything, which is frustrating me to no end. The bar exam is coming up quickly, and I feel more unprepared now than ever.

I'm sitting on the couch, rereading the same paragraph for the millionth time as I desperately try to keep my eyelids from closing.

"Why don't you go take a nap?" Brandon suggests.

"I can't. I need to finish this chapter, and then I have to fold the laundry."

"You can barely hold your head up." Brandon reaches over and pulls the book off my lap. "I think you should make an appointment at the doctor."

"Why?" I ask, my voice coming out too high-pitched.

"You haven't been feeling well since we were in Russia."

"It's just the stress of Alex and Natalie's kidnapping and the bar exam. I'll be okay once all this is over," I say, hoping my answer sounds convincing.

"I don't think—"

My phone rings. I answer it quickly, thankful for the distraction. "Hey, girlfriend. How did your appointment go?"

Natalie had her check-up with the obstetrician this afternoon. I've been waiting all day to hear if the issues with her placenta have been resolved.

"Everything's great. I got the all-clear." Natalie breathes an audible sigh of relief.

"That's awesome." I put my hand over the phone to tell Brandon the good news. "Does that mean you'll be leaving us to visit your parents?"

"Alex is booking the flight now. Are you and Brandon free to come over for dinner tonight?"

"Hang on, let me ask." I turn to Brandon. "They want to know if we're available to have dinner with them tonight."

"Are you up to it?"

"I am," I smile reassuringly.

Brandon hesitates for a long second before answering, "Yes, we can be there."

"We're free. What time?"

"About seven-ish," Natalie suggests.

"We'll be there." Quickly, I add, "Have you talked to my parents?"

"No, why?"

"I was just curious."

"Can we pick this up later? We have a few errands to run before dinner."

"Sounds like a plan to me. Talk to you later."

After we hang up, I set my phone aside and turn to Brandon. "May I have my book back, please?"

He keeps a hold on it. "I'm concerned about you, Svetlana."

"Bran—"

"No." He stands. His dominant presence looms over me. "You don't ever stop. If you aren't cleaning, you're cooking. If you aren't cooking, you're studying. You need a break, *papillon*."

Brandon tosses the book onto the sofa and takes my hands, pulling me up from the couch. "I want you to go and rest."

"But—"

"Don't *but* me." He points to the steps. "You will go lay down. I'll finish the laundry."

"Yes, Sir." I relent, knowing he's not going to budge on this. "Will you come with me?"

"If I come to bed with you, you won't get any rest." He leans in and kisses my forehead. "Go. I'll wake you in a bit."

Brandon

Lana pouts as she slowly walks up the steps. It seems whatever she picked up in Russia is still hanging on, and I'm getting concerned. Staying behind was supposed to be so she could rest, but then her uncle showed up, and any idea of rest went right out the window.

Svetlana was determined to be the perfect hostess. When she explained how long it'd been since she last saw her uncle, I took a step back and allowed it. But it's time to put my foot down before she collapses from exhaustion. While she rests, I fold the laundry and unload the dishwasher.

Alex: Do you have a minute?

Me: Yeah, what's up?

Alex: Are you alone?

Me: I am.

He's being oddly cryptic, especially since I'll see him in a few hours.

Alex: I'm planning a surprise wedding for Natalie while we're in Northmeadow.

Me: How can I help?

Alex: Don't tell Lana until after tonight. I'll get you more info as soon as I have it. Just make sure you both will be there.

Me: I wouldn't miss it for the world.

Maybe I should be more surprised by Alex's text, but I'm not. I knew that after how close he came to losing her in Mexico, he wouldn't want to wait to get married. However, it's another thing that'll get in our way. I hoped to talk Lana into telling Alex and Natalie about our engagement tonight. But in light of this news, she wouldn't agree to it.

Knowing I proposed and Lana said yes, but being unable to tell anyone is hard. Selfishly, I want to put the ring back on her finger and tell the world she's agreed to be my wife. But I get why she wants to hold off. Alex and Natalie lived through hell at Moreno's hands. It's only fair that all the attention should be on them right now.

After booking our flight to Missouri, I go into our bedroom. Svetlana's curled up on my side of the bed. Her hair is splayed out on my pillow, and her hands are tucked under her cheek as she snores softly—something I'll never tell her about. She looks so peaceful that I hate to wake her. But if I know her, she'll want some time to get ready before we have to leave.

Sitting on the edge of the bed, I gently shake her shoulder. "Lana. It's time to wake up."

"I don't want to." She swats my hand away.

"Says the girl who argued about napping," I chuckle.

Lana rolls onto her back, and her eyes flutter open. Her hands wrap around my neck, pulling me to her. "Do we have time before we leave?"

I look at my wrist, pretending there's a watch. "We should be fine," I say as I pull the sheet down and find her nude underneath. I swirl my tongue around her nipple, and she moans softly.

With my free hand, I open my pants and shrug them down my legs. I crawl up between her legs, kissing my way as I go. Then, I bury my face in her pussy and lick her clit gently. She moans louder and grinds against my face. I put my arms under her thighs and lift her ass to get better access.

I bite her clit lightly, and she cries out in pleasure. "You're dripping for me," I say as I slide two fingers inside her fucking her hard and fast.

She bucks her hips against my face. "Oh God, Brandon. That feels so good. Please don't stop," she begs.

I keep up my pace and feel her pussy tighten around my fingers. I push them deeper inside, hooking them to hit the spot that drives her wild. I move my tongue faster and suck her clit harder.

She cries out, and her back arches as she explodes in my arms. I continue sucking her clit and pumping my fingers, drawing out her orgasm. I don't stop until every last ripple has stopped, and she lies panting on the bed.

I pull my fingers out and sit back on my knees. Lana watches with lust-filled eyes as I lick her juices from my fingers.

"Turn over and get on your knees," I command.

I rub the head of my dick through her pussy, teasing her overly sensitive clit. She wiggles her ass, trying to get me to hurry. My hand lands with a crack, and she yelps. Without warning, I slide my cock into her pussy and my finger into her ass and begin to move. With my other hand on her hips, fuck her hard and fast.

Reaching around, I pinch a nipple as I thrust into her. Lana moans loudly. I slam my cock deep inside and hold it there.

"I'm so close. Don't stop, Sir."

I chuckle. "Your wish is my command."

Pulling my finger out of her ass, I grab her hips and pound my cock into her as fast as I can. Her pussy tightens around my cock, and I explode deep inside her. When I pull out, cum drips from between her legs, and fuck me, my cock twitches in arousal. But we're out of time. If we don't get dressed now, we won't leave the house tonight.

I watch Lana as she and Natalie ooh and ahh while looking at the ultrasound photos.

"It's hard to believe you're going to be a father in a few months."

"You're telling me. Fatherhood was never in my plans, but I wouldn't change a thing," Alex says, not taking his eyes off his soon-to-be wife. "The second Natalie told me she was pregnant, everything shifted."

"I can't even imagine."

"Just wait. Lana will get the baby bug now. We'll be raising our kids together," he chuckles.

Raising children together? Alex and I have been through many things, but much like him, I never envisioned us having kids. Now that he's said it, I can't wait to put a baby inside Lana and watch her body grow and change as she gives our future child life. A little girl with light brown skin and long curly hair. Or perhaps a little boy with Lana's blue eyes.

"This is so good." Natalie groans after taking a mouthful of noodles and vegetables.

Lana laughs. "I've never seen you enjoy food so much."

"I am eating for two." She smiles and places her hand on her little round tummy.

"Lana said you two are leaving for Missouri this weekend. How long are you staying?" I ask.

"Only a few weeks," Alex answers. "We promised Charlotte she could have a small bridal shower while we're there."

"Has she settled down about the baby yet?" Lana asks, rolling her eyes.

"Kind of." Natalie gestures with her chopsticks while she talks. "Mainly, she avoids the topic, and that's fine. Right now, I don't need any more stress."

"Do I get to throw you a proper Russian shower before your wedding?" Lana asks.

"Of course." Natalie pauses and looks between us. "Can you

two come to Northmeadow? You're my maid of honor. You should be at the shower."

Lana looks at me for permission. "The bar is coming up fast. Are you sure you can take the time away from studying?" I ask, raising an eyebrow. I don't give her a chance to respond before answering, "We'll talk about it and get back to you."

"Are you done?" Natalie asks Alex before taking his plate.

"Yes, baby girl," he says before turning to me. "How about we move to the living room while the girls clean up?"

I follow Alex into the other room. "Did Max call you guys yet?" I ask quietly.

"He called earlier this evening."

"So, you know about them adopting that Amelia kid?"

"We do. Natalie was ecstatic." He glances into the kitchen where the girls are whispering and giggling. "She's really attached to her. I think it'll be good for them," Alex says thoughtfully. "Amelia's not a replacement for Jelena, but it might help to fill the hole left in their hearts."

"I think you might be right."

"What did Lana think about it?" he asks.

"She was thrilled. Once she's more settled, I'm hoping we can fly home and spend some time getting to know her."

The girls come into the living room, chatting about bridal showers, babies, and weddings. Alex excuses himself.

When he comes back, he's holding up a manilla folder. "This is the real reason I asked you over tonight." He takes his seat next to Natalie.

"What is it?" Alex pulls some papers from the folder and passes them to me. He and Natalie are silent while I quickly skim them. "You're kidding, right?" I ask, looking up in complete disbelief. With shaky hands, I set the papers on the glass coffee table.

"I'm dead serious."

"What is it?" Lana asks.

"Alex wants to step down from his company, and he wants me to take over as the CEO," I say in disbelief.

"Are you kidding?" Lana looks between Alex and Natalie.

"I'm not kidding," Alex says, taking Natalie's hand in his. "We're planning to start a new venture together."

I don't know what to make of any of this. Alex is routine and patterned. It's completely out of character for him to make rash decisions or to change course abruptly. I'm concerned that what happened in Mexico messed with his head more than anyone realized. "Care to elaborate?"

Alex takes a deep breath before announcing, "We're opening Jelena's Hope NYC."

I don't know what I expected, but that wasn't it. "I don't know what to say."

"All you have to say is yes and sign the contract." Alex pulls out a pen and slides it across the table.

"Aren't you afraid this might put a target on your back?" Lana asks, concerned.

"Judging by recent events, I think the target is already there. But for this, there'll be state-of-the-art security in place." I pick up the pen and click it nervously, listening to Alex explain. "Dimitri's already on it. So, I have no doubts about our safety." He pauses and looks at me expectantly. "The new position comes with a raise. If that helps sweeten the deal."

Lifting the papers from the table, I make a big show of flipping through each page until I reach the last one with the blank line waiting for my signature. Putting pen to paper, I sign my name and then look up. "I would have signed either way."

We all share a laugh.

"What does the timetable look like?" I ask, curious to hear his vision for the transition.

"I plan to speak to the employees and contact my personal clients over the next few weeks." Alex leans forward to sign the contract. It isn't until he's done that his body visibly relaxes. "By the six-week mark, the transition will be complete."

I didn't see this coming, but given the circumstances, it makes perfect sense. We've been involved with Maxim and his fight against trafficking for years, but it's always been more of a passive involvement. Everything we did was from the safety of our New York office or Max's home. We were removed from the true horror of trafficking.

Moreno taking Alex and Natalie has been life-altering for everyone, especially for Alex. He hasn't said much about what they endured, but I've heard about the ruthless nature of Moreno and his men. I also know Alex had a hand in Moreno's demise. It goes without saying that their lives are irrevocably changed.

Unfortunately, trafficking will never go away. As long as that sad reality remains, places like Jelena's Hope will be necessary. Having a facility like this in New York City will be a great resource. Alex walking away from the company he worked so hard to build is a significant life change. Doing so to open Jelena's Hope here in the city is an even bigger leap toward being more actively involved in Maxim's business.

"That sounds doable."

"Are you planning on working at the center, Nat?" Lana asks.

"We haven't talked about all the details." Natalie looks at Alex. "But yes, I plan to be on the staff as much as I'm able."

"I'm so proud of you. You could've let your experience in Mexico ruin you, but instead, you're going to change so many lives because of it," Lana says, clearly in awe of her best friend's bravery.

"It hasn't been easy," Natalie says quietly. "I know Silverio's dead, but the memories can be so vivid—so real. Every day, sometimes more than once a day, I have to make a conscious decision not to let the memories get the best of me." Alex wraps an arm around his wife as she wipes a tear from her cheek. "I have to be stronger than the memories."

"I know a little about that," Lana says. "Obviously, not in the same way, but if you want to talk about it, I'm here."

Natalie gives a slight nod and rests her head against Alex's shoulder.

The web of human trafficking is a sinister force that preys on the vulnerable and has mercilessly robbed countless people of their dreams and aspirations. Svetlana's life was completely changed by this dark reality, leaving scars that will never fully heal. Max and Irina faced a heart-wrenching tragedy when Jelena was forcefully taken away, erasing all their plans for her future. Yet, a twist of fate granted them the chance to restore a young girl's stolen life.

My gaze drifts across the room, settling on Alex and Natalie, knowing how close they almost came to losing everything. Their story reminds me that not everyone is as lucky. Although invisible scars may forever mark their hearts, they've chosen not to let anger consume them, choosing resilience over resignation. Instead, they've embraced their roles as champions against the very forces that once sought to crush them.

Alex embodies courage in its purest form. He's the bravest man I know and someone I strive to be more like. And Natalie, I'm in awe of the personal growth she's experienced in such a short time. They refuse to turn their heads and assume someone else will deal with the problem. Because of people like them, I believe in the promise of a better future.

Svetlana

WHEN BRANDON TOLD ME ALEX WAS PLANNING A surprise wedding for Natalie, I assumed a small, understated ceremony at the local courthouse. I was wrong. He wants the whole experience. I've spent hours texting back and forth with him, Anthony, and Charlotte.

"Yes, Mrs. Clarke. I'm certain Natalie wanted the dark purple orchids," I say patiently. "I can send you the pictures again."

"I'm sorry to be such a pain, dear. Since Natalie isn't getting a say in all this, I want to be sure everything is perfect."

Natalie's mother has never been my favorite person. I don't think that's a secret. She was downright awful to Natalie with the whole Tommy thing. Natalie forgives far easier than I do, but I'm biting my tongue and trying to keep my personal feelings out of it. This is my best friend's wedding. I only care that it's everything she's ever dreamt about.

"I understand."

Charlotte continues complaining. "Leo's been sending me pictures." Charlotte continues complaining. "But Stanley and I haven't been able to be at the lake to oversee anything."

"He's sending them to me too. Natalie's going to love it."

"How long until you get there?"

"We're pulling in now."

"Natalie's coming. I have to go," Charlotte whispers.

"See you later." I chuckle and disconnect the call.

"You're being very patient with her," Brandon says as we exit the car.

"I'm not going to lie. Charlotte's a lot." I follow him up the path to the house. "But she's Natalie's mother, so I'm trying to behave."

"Can you zip my dress, Sir?" I ask Brandon when he comes out of the bathroom.

"I can." He steps closer to me, his warm breath on my neck as he slides the zipper up. "I already can't wait to unzip it."

"Unfortunately, that won't be tonight. You'll be staying in Viktor's cottage with the other guys."

Brandon groans. "Don't remind me."

"Are you two ready?" Alex calls from outside the door. "They'll be here any minute."

Brandon opens the door while I slide my shoes on. "We're good to go."

"Am I doing the right thing?" Alex asks nervously. "Maybe this is too much?"

"It's too late to be asking that."

Alex's eyes widen as he looks at me over Brandon's shoulder.

"They're pulling in now," Tony calls from the kitchen.

"She's going to love it," Brandon says and clasps his shoulder. "Let's go get you to your girl."

We part ways when we get to the main area of the house. While Alex hurries to the front door to intercept Natalie, we go out the back door to join the rest of the guests who are having drinks and hors d'oeuvres.

"For you, *papillon*." Brandon offers me a glass of Chardonnay.

If I decline, he's going to question my actions. "Thank you." I accept the drink and bring it to my lips, only taking a tiny sip.

It's only a few minutes before Alex and Natalie step out onto the patio. Although I can't hear what they're saying, I can see the confused look on Natalie's face. Finally, Alex takes Natalie by the hand and leads her to where we're all waiting.

I set my drink down and hurry over, wrapping my arms around the bride-to-be. "Can you believe he did this?"

"I'm still trying to process everything," she says as she hugs me. "Were you in on this too?"

"I was," I answer proudly.

"Before we start our meal," Alex says, getting everyone's attention. "I want to take a moment to express my gratitude. I would never have pulled this off on my own. Even with such short notice, you've all helped create something incredible. Without each one of you, none of this would be possible. From the bottom of my heart, I thank you."

"Please take your seats, and the meal will be served," Anthony instructs.

We enjoy a leisurely al fresco dinner. The mood is light and carefree as the sun gracefully begins to dip below the horizon. Despite the idyllic evening, memories of the last time we were all here threaten to intrude on the present moment. I make a conscious effort to push those thoughts aside. This is about the present and the future. I refuse to allow the horrible events of the past to overshadow this celebration.

As the evening winds down, the number of remaining guests grows smaller.

"Excuse us, please," Alex says as he and Natalie walk her parents to their car.

Once they're out of earshot, Luna asks, "How exactly did they meet?"

Brandon and I look at each other and laugh. "Who gets to tell the story?"

"You can," Brandon says, shaking his head. "I told it last time."

"Good." I rub my hands together. It wasn't funny the night it all happened, but it's since become one of my favorite stories to tell. "When I first met Natalie, she was a shy, backward girl who could barely utter the word sex."

"You're not serious, are you?" Luna asks in disbelief.

"She's dead serious." Brandon jumps in. "Lana and I had dated for a few years before I met Natalie."

"So, Brandon and I planned this CNC scene a weekend when Natalie was supposed to be out of town. I was naked and cuffed to the bed when she came home unexpectedly and walked in on what she thought was an assault. She called the NYPD—"

"What did we miss?" Alex asks as he and Natalie appear from around the corner of the cottage.

"Lana's just telling us how Natalie first learned about the life-style," Luna says, trying to hold back a laugh.

Natalie looks at me with her best angry face. "I was hoping she would've forgotten that by now,"

"How could we ever forget that?" Brandon chuckles, then turns back to Luna. "I thought for sure I'd be calling Alex to bail me out."

After I finish telling everyone about Brandon's brush with the law, we fast-forward to the night I invited Natalie to the club for the first time. I skip the parts about the private room and the flogger—Sam doesn't need to know the details.

When I'm done, Sam tells us some childhood stories about Alex. It seems he was always a serious, detail-oriented person.

Natalie yawns and snuggles up next to Alex for a second before he announces, "We're going inside. My bride-to-be is ready for bed."

"We should all turn in." Sam yawns and stretches. "Tomorrow's going to be a big day."

"Girls in one house, boys in the other." I jump from my seat.

"Says who?" Alex asks, laughing.

The original plan was to have a traditional wedding shower. Mama and I were going to make Russian *korovai*. We were going to have Alex take part in the tradition of *vykup nevesty*—paying a ransom for his bride. Since he decided to have a surprise wedding, all those plans went out the window. But I'm getting my way with this. The bride and groom *will* spend tonight apart.

I put my hand on my hips and cock one out to the side. "You can't see the bride on her wedding day until the ceremony."

"You have a bossy little sub there, Brand."

"She can be bratty at times." Brandon smacks my ass, and I shriek. "But she's right. Time to say goodnight. You can't see Natalie until the wedding."

"Some friends you are." Alex makes a show of rolling his eyes and takes Natalie by the hand. "Come on, baby girl. I'll walk you to our bedroom door, and we'll say our goodnights."

"Viktor, maybe you should stand guard in case he tries to sneak into her room," Brandon jokes.

Alex flips Brandon off as he and Natalie disappear inside the house, leaving the rest of us laughing.

While they say their goodnights, the rest of us start cleaning up.

"Do you think you and Brandon will walk down the aisle next?" Luna sidles up to me as I collect the empty drinks.

"Us? Oh, I don't know." I feign innocence.

"I know love when I see it," she says. "That boy is in love with you."

"What about you and Sam? You've been together for a long time."

Luna watches Sam, who's talking to Anthony and Leo. "Sam is my Dominant, but there will never be anything else. He made that clear when we first met."

"Never say never." I smile, hoping to encourage her.

Sam motions to her. "I'll be back," she says and walks away.

While Anthony extinguishes the fire, Leo comes to help me finish cleaning up the last of the cups that are strewn around the sitting area. When we're done, we sit down and go over some details for the morning. Our heads swing to the house where Alex has just shut the patio doors rather forcefully.

"He looks like a lost puppy," I whisper, and Leo laughs.

"Night, everyone. Come along, kids," Luna says, motioning for Leo and me to follow her. "Let's go find the bride."

"He gets to stay in the house?" Alex whines.

"He's just one of the girls," Tony jokes.

I thread my arm through Leo's and grin at Alex as we walk past him. Even though he's acting like a spoiled toddler, he's a big boy. It's only one night without Natalie.

Svetlana

It's Natalie's wedding day. We're just getting our gowns on, and I'm already exhausted. We've been going nonstop since we got up this morning.

Me: I think I want to elope.

Brandon: Why?

Me: This is insanity. I want it to be just you and me. We can tell everyone after it's done.

Brandon: *Papillon*, I'll gladly marry you in whatever kind of ceremony you wish.

Me: I'll see you at the end of the aisle.

After I hit send, I realize what I said and how much I wish it were Brandon and me getting married today. And once again, I find myself pushing unwanted thoughts back down where they belong so I can focus on the present.

My dress is stunning. It's a floor-length dark purple chiffon gown that sits off the shoulder. I step into it and reach behind me to zip it, but I can't quite get it. Holding it against me, I open the bathroom door.

"Can you help me with my dress, Mrs. Clarke?"

"Sure, honey. Turn around." She zips up my dress and says, "You look stunning."

"Brandon's going to go crazy. You'll be walking down the aisle next," Natalie says, and I see the dreamy look in her eyes.

"I don't think so. Marriage is not in my plans." What? Why in the world did I say that? I want to marry Brandon.

"Not in your plans? What do you mean, dear?" Charlotte asks.

"Natalie, can you help me with my bowtie?" Leo gives me a questioning look.

"Let's see what I can do. Sit down."

Thankfully, there's a knock on the door, and Charlotte's attention is shifted away from me.

"Luna, don't you look beautiful," she says, stepping aside to let her in.

"And you are a gorgeous mother of the bride."

"Speaking of the bride, I think it's time we get her dressed." I get the hanger with Natalie's vintage dress and lay it on the bed.

"I'll step outside while you change," Leo says, earning an approving smile from Charlotte.

Carefully, I unzip the gown and hold it as Natalie steps in. She unties her robe and tosses it onto the bed. "Those pearls are so hot. It's a good thing Alex won't know what's underneath until later," I say when I see her lingerie.

"Svetlana," Charlotte scolds me.

"Sorry, Mrs. C." I shrug. "But it's the truth. He's going to go crazy when he undresses her tonight."

Charlotte's cheeks turn a deep red. Luna slaps my arm, making me laugh.

"Saved by the bell," I say in a sing-song voice when my phone starts ringing. Mrs. Clarke steps into my place, helping Natalie get dressed while I grab my phone.

My eyes fill with tears when I see Papa's picture on the screen. One minute I'm happy. The next, I'm crying and saying ridiculous things. These darn hormones. I blink them away and answer the call, putting it on speaker.

"How is my little girl today?" Papa's voice is warm and affectionate.

"I'm good, Papa," I reply with a smile.

"Turn on your camera. Mama and I want to see your dress," Papa insists eagerly.

"Svetlana. You look beautiful," Mama remarks with pride.

"Thanks, Mama." I turn the camera around. "Say hi to everyone."

A chorus of hellos fills the room, adding to the excitement.

"Natalia. You are a most stunning bride. I wish we could be there to celebrate with you today," Papa expresses wistfully.

"So do I," Natalie responds.

"I'll have them on video the whole time. They won't miss a second."

"Hi, Natalie." Amelia pops into view. She looks so much happier than the last time I spoke to her.

"Hi, sweetheart." Natalie's face lights up. "How's everything going?"

"I'm starting to get used to it here. Miss Irina is teaching me Russian, or at least trying to." She scrunches her face.

"I hope you do better than I have." Russian is not an easy language to learn. I can manage a few words to get by, but mostly I rely on Alex to do the talking for me.

"You look like a princess, Natalie."

"Thank you."

"When will I get to see you?"

"I'm not sure. We'll talk to Max and Irina and see what they can do, okay?"

"Yep. Gotta go."

"I have to finish getting ready. I don't want to be late for my own wedding." Natalie laughs nervously.

"*Pozdravlyayem vas oboikh I nadeyemsya, chto u vas budet mnogo schastlivykh let vmeste,*" Papa says.

Natalie looks at me to translate.

"He said congratulations to both of you. And they hope you have many happy years together."

"Thank you, both."

I promise to call them when the ceremony starts and hang up.

"I can't believe I'm about to marry Alex."

"And it's all thanks to me," I say proudly.

Natalie takes my hands in hers. "I'm so grateful you asked me to go to Fire and Ice with you that night," she whispers, her eyes filling with tears.

"We just spent hours getting our makeup done. There will be no tears yet." I wave her off, not because I'm not equally as thankful but because I don't want to start crying, too.

"It's time to put your veil on. Come sit down." Charlotte directs Natalie to a chair, where she sets the exquisite crystal tiara on her head, pinning it so it doesn't fall off. The photographer's camera clicks furiously, capturing every second.

"It's exactly what I wanted. How did you know?"

"Aren't you glad I know your Pinterest password?" Natalie and I both laugh.

After exchanging the traditional old, new, borrowed, and blue treasures, it's time to go. I hold the train of Natalie's dress over my arm so it doesn't catch on the floor as we walk through the cottage.

We're still posing for pictures when the front door opens, and Viktor walks in. Everyone else is oblivious, but I watch Natalie turn around. Viktor freezes mid-step and swipes his hand over his shiny bald head before he catches himself. "You're the most perfect bride. Alex is a lucky man." He leans in and kisses her cheek before clearing his throat. "We're ready to start."

"We're ready, too," I say a little too loudly after witnessing the oddly tender interaction.

"I'll see you out there." Viktor studies Natalie a minute longer before walking outside.

I step up next to Natalie. "If I didn't know better—"

"Don't," she says, not letting me finish my thought. "We've been through a lot together, that's all."

"Whatever." I roll my eyes. Viktor never lets his feelings slip, but this time, he did, and I saw. He's in love with Natalie.

Before I can think about it anymore, Leo throws open the French doors. "Time to go, ladies."

Brandon

Maxim called several weeks after the wedding and asked me to fly out to Russia. There was business that needed to be done in person and couldn't wait any longer. Amelia was living with them full-time and eagerly anticipated her adoption. Since she and Lana were introduced, they video chat every night and have been looking forward to spending time together.

Lana was all set to travel, but the firm she was interning with assigned her to another criminal case. She's competing against other highly qualified candidates for a full-time position with this firm. So, at the last minute, she had to back out of the trip. As disappointed as I was, I understand Lana's just starting her career and can't afford to let opportunities like this pass her by.

While I'm in Russia, I'm also planning to take the opportunity to speak to Maxim. I want to do this right and ask for his blessing to marry Svetlana. Now that Alex and Natalie are happily married, it's time for Lana and me to move forward with announcing our engagement.

With the ring box in my pocket, I walk through the sprawling estate and find Misha at his post. The office doors closed. "Is the boss busy?" I ask.

"He's going through some emails he received this morning."

"Can you see if he has a few minutes? I want to talk to him about something."

"Go right in," Misha says and opens the door.

"Brandon." Maxim looks over his laptop screen at me. "I was not expecting you."

"There's something I need to discuss with you."

He closes his computer. "Please, have a seat."

My legs are wobbly as I take tentative steps into the room, and my voice comes out shaky as I say, "Yes, sir."

"What is wrong?" he asks, alarmed.

"Nothing's wrong." I sit on the edge of one of the antique wing-backed chairs across from his desk. I've sat here many times before and never felt fear—even at times I probably should've. But today, I'm terrified.

"What can I do for you?" He folds his hands on the desk in front of him.

"I'd like to speak with you about Svetlana."

"Go on."

"As you know, we've been dating for several years." I practiced this speech in my room all morning to ensure I didn't screw up any of the details. I knew exactly how many years it had been, but now that it's happening, my thoughts are scattered. My mind is blank. Everything I'd so carefully rehearsed is gone. It's a struggle to get coherent words out of my mouth. "I care about her very much."

"Care about her?" he asks, raising an eyebrow.

"I... I more than care." I stumble over my words. "I love her."

Maxim studies me with a discerning gaze. He stays quiet for a long moment, and I'm unsure if it's to process my declaration or to give me time to relax. When I don't say anything, he nods and gestures with his hand for me to continue.

I take a deep breath and wipe my sweaty palms on my pants, trying to summon the courage to speak. And hoping when I do, that I sound more like a grown man than a bumbling teenage boy.

The room seems to shrink around me as I search for the right words to convey the depth of my emotions. "You know my history." Maxim nods. "For most of my adult life, I punished myself for my past sins. I didn't believe I was worthy to have another submissive. Deserving the love of a woman wasn't even a consideration. I was prepared to go through life alone until the night Svetlana walked into Alex's kitchen," I say, finally finding my stride. "Svetlana's brought purpose to my life. I've worked hard to be deserving of her love."

Maxim's expression softens, his stern demeanor giving way to a glimmer of understanding. He may be a tough Bratva boss and a strict Dominant, but he's also a man who, after nearly forty years of marriage, is still very much in love with his wife. When I speak of the meaning Lana's brought to my life, I know Max understands exactly what I'm talking about.

"Svetlana's shown me the true meaning of love. Together, we've built a foundation of trust and respect. She completes me in ways I never thought possible." My voice cracks with emotion. "I can't imagine a future without her. I want to spend the rest of my life with Svetlana." I stop and swallow over the lump in my throat. "I'm asking for your blessing to ask Svetlana to be my wife."

A moment of silence hangs in the air as Maxim seems to be absorbing what I've asked. "Russian tradition is that the male suitor brings gifts to the prospective young lady's family," he says, watching me expectantly.

Oh shit. I didn't research what traditions there might be. "I'm afraid I didn't come prepared." I move to stand, ready to leave the office, knowing I've lost my chance.

"Sit." Max's voice booms, and I drop back onto the chair. Then, a smile spreads across his face, "Love is a powerful force. It can bring both immense joy and formidable challenge." He leans forward, his expression revealing a mixture of emotions—pride, concern, and a flicker of paternal warmth. "I have witnessed the love you have for my daughter. You have remained by her side, supporting her through triumph and trial. You have my blessing to marry *moya babochka.*"

Relief washes over me, knowing I have his approval. "Thank you, sir."

Maxim stands and rounds his desk. "Let us go find Irina to tell her the joyous news, *moy syn.*"

My heart's full of gratitude, knowing this moment marks the beginning of a new chapter in my life—a chapter that will be filled with love and happiness for Svetlana and me.

It's early evening in Russian, about midnight in New York, when I sneak away to call Lana. We talk this time every night, so she'll be expecting my call. I bring up her contact and tap the green connect button. There's a slight delay before the line rings. Instead of Svetlana answering, it goes to voicemail. I try again and get the same result.

Me: Are you there?

With my phone in hand, I wait to see the text switch from *delivered* to *read,* but it doesn't happen. It's not like her to be unreachable. For a moment, I panic, anticipating the worst. Then, it dawns on me—she must've fallen asleep early. I told her she was working herself into exhaustion.

Me: It seems you're sleeping. I'm glad to know you're finally taking my advice. Rest up, *mon papillon.* I'll be on a plane back to you tomorrow morning. We have three weeks apart to make up for.

I slide the phone into my pocket and return to Maxim's office to finish up the file I'm working on. This unnamed contact in Yemen and their group are working to crack a child trafficking ring, something not uncommon in that region, that's said to have nearly one hundred children—boys and girls.

They're planning to intercept what's supposed to be an outbound shipment heading for Saudi Arabia. It's a complicated and dangerous mission, but with so many children's lives on the line, there's no room for failure. If they make a mistake and the traffickers get the children out of Yemen, we may never be able to find them.

While Maxim coordinates the details of the rescue mission, I'm making calls to secure beds in treatment centers for the children. Once they're safe, the work begins to find out who they are and if they have families searching for them or if their families are responsible for their current situation.

As I round the corner, I nearly collide with Misha. "I was just coming to find you. The boss needs you in the situation room." We hurry down the hall as he explains, "There was a leak. The *ublyudoks* discovered the plan and attempted to move the *deti* early."

"Fuck. How far did they get?"

"They made it through three checkpoints. They're within a half hour of the border."

If they make it across the border, the children will disappear. "Do we still have a chance?" I ask as we arrive at the room. But Misha doesn't have a chance to answer. As we step across the threshold, I see what looks like a small war playing out on the large screen hanging on the wall. Shots ring out. Men are yelling in languages I don't understand. "What the hell happened?"

"There was a traitor in the group. The traffickers moved early," Dimitri explains without taking his eyes off the monitors.

A child's piercing scream silences everyone in the room. We watch in horror as a little body falls lifeless to the ground. My stomach roils, and I fight the urge to vomit.

We're silent for the duration of the fight. I don't know how long it is before the gunshots cease and the dust begins to clear. On the ground are several men lying in pools of blood. In the background are the sounds of terrified children crying.

Max's phone rings. "*Zdravstvuyte. Day mne podrobnosti. Chert voz'mi.*"

"What's he saying?"

"He's asking for the details," Dimitri explains and listens. He continues to translate for me. "The leak was caught and is being dealt with. Five children were injured but not seriously." His shoulders fall. "Two children lost their lives."

A heaviness settles in the room.

Maxim finishes his phone call. Without a word, he stands, pushing his chair out so forcefully it falls over. With heavy strides, he leaves the room, slamming the door behind him.

I turn to follow him, but Timur grabs my arm. "You're best to give him space. He won't be in a good head space right now."

I look between Timur and the closed door. "I'll take my chances. I don't think he should be alone."

The office door is cracked open. Max is standing with his hand on the window. His shoulders are hunched, and his head is down. Quietly, I step into his space, closing the door behind me.

"Tell Misha to call and have my jet ready. It's time for you to return to New York," he says without turning around.

"I'm sorry," I say quietly, but I know my words do little to quell the anger and helplessness Max is experiencing right now. The same helplessness we're all feeling.

"What happened is unacceptable. We must do better." His arm drops to his side, and he turns to face me. "We cannot lose another child."

"I'll let Svetlana know my trip has been extended." My declaration leaves no room for argument. "Where do we start in tightening up our forces and ensuring there are no more traitors among us? Tell me what to do and where to go."

"I appreciate you making yourself available for a longer time," Maxim says. "However, your work begins and ends in this room. I cannot have you directly involved. Svetlana's life has already been tainted by too much danger."

"I want to take a bigger role," I argue. "I can do that while ensuring she's safe."

"No." Maxim slices his hand through the air. "I appreciate

your eagerness to do more, but I will not allow it. I cannot let you take any greater risks."

"But—"

"There are no buts. If you wish to maintain my blessing over your union with Svetlana, you will respect my decision."

I want to continue to argue. To make him see things my way, but the resolute look on his face makes it clear no matter what I say, he won't budge. "I understand and will respect your authority."

"Thank you. Now, we must get busy. There is much work to be done."

It's going to be a long and busy night. Before we get to work, I text Lana, letting her know my trip home has been delayed and that I won't be leaving Russia for a few more days. Then, I rejoin Max and Dimitri in the tech room. Misha and Timur have already begun arranging safe transport for the children to treatment facilities.

Predatels, traitors, will be dealt with in the harshest of ways. Death will not be swift. The men responsible for tonight's events are in the custody of our Yemen contact. Their fate is being spread throughout the various channels. Hopefully, the message is loud enough and strong enough to discourage anyone else from double-crossing us.

This job is mentally and emotionally draining. By the time we wrap up for the night, I'm barely able to drag myself to my room, where I collapse in bed. I check my phone again, but there's still nothing from Lana. I lose the fight to stay awake. My eyes close, and I drift off into a restless sleep.

Svetlana

"Do you want me to stay with you?" Pyotr asks as we exit the hospital elevator.

"It's my yearly gynecology appointment. I think I can manage on my own."

"I'll wait downstairs in the main lobby then. Text me when you're done."

"Will do." I smile and walk through the glass doors leading to the doctor's office.

I'm actually here for my first pregnancy visit, but Pyotr doesn't know about the baby yet. It felt wrong to tell anyone before Brandon knew. I held off on telling him before he left for Russia, knowing that if I did, he wouldn't have gone, and Papa needed him. He was supposed to be home a few nights ago, but unfortunately, the rescue mission went terribly wrong.

I'm disappointed that he's not here with me today to hear the baby's heartbeat. I plan to record it and play it for him when I tell him I'm pregnant.

"Can I help you?" the receptionist asks.

"I have an appointment with Dr. Young."

"Your name?"

"Svetlana Solonik."

The keys on her keyboard click as she types in my information. "It looks like I have everything I need." She looks up and smiles. "If you have a seat, he'll be right with you."

The waiting room is cozy, with only about ten seats. There are two other visibly pregnant women there. One of them is engrossed in her phone. The other is flipping through the pages of a magazine. She looks up, and we exchange smiles as I take a seat. I'm suffering from a mix of nerves and excitement. Trying to keep myself busy while I wait, I pick up a magazine with a picture of a mother cradling her newborn. It's a tender interaction and one I can't wait to share with my own baby. I flip through the glossy pages, but I'm unable to concentrate long enough to read any of the articles.

The door to the patient rooms opens, and a woman wearing light blue scrubs steps out. "Svetlana?"

My legs tremble as I walk across the room to meet her. "That's me."

"My name's Jill. I'll be taking your vitals today," she says as we walk to the triage area. "How have you been feeling?"

"Actually, I'm feeling quite well."

"No morning sickness?"

"It seems to have gone away," I answer, thankful I'm no longer vomiting.

She takes my weight and blood pressure before escorting me to an exam room. "Dr. Young's finishing with another patient. He'll be with you shortly."

While I wait, I pull out my phone and scroll my secret Baby Carpenter board on Pinterest. The day I learned I was pregnant, I started searching for baby shower decorations and nursery ideas. I can't wait to convert the guest bedroom across from our room into our baby's nursery. I'm hoping Brandon will be okay with it being traditional in style with elements of Russian design.

There's a quick knock before the door opens. "Good afternoon, Lana. How are you today?"

"I'm doing well."

"Are you ready to have a listen?"

"I am," I say excitedly. "Do you mind if I record the baby's heartbeat for my fiancé? He couldn't be here today."

"That's perfectly fine with me." Dr. Young smiles kindly. "Can I have you lie back and pull your shirt up?"

While he gets the doppler ready, I do as he requests and move my shirt to expose my stomach. Then, I open the recording app on my phone. Dr. Young squirts some warm gel on my lower abdomen and places the probe against my skin. There's staticky noise as he moves it around, but nothing that sounds like a heartbeat.

"Sometimes, these little ones can be tricky to find."

"Is everything okay?" I ask nervously.

"Early in pregnancy, locating the heartbeat with the doppler can be difficult." He removes the instrument. "I'm going to get the ultrasound machine for a better look. Excuse me for a minute."

The doctor leaves the room, and for the first time, I wish I asked Pyotr to stay with me. Dr. Young has been my physician since I moved to New York City. However, being here for an obstetrician visit feels intimidating. Rather than being excited, I'm feeling scared.

"Alrighty," the doctor says when he returns, wheeling a big machine in front of him. "This should do the trick."

He puts more gel directly onto my stomach, and the machine flickers to life. A tiny bean-shaped image appears on the screen. "Is that my baby?"

"Mhm," he mumbles as he moves the probe around and clicks buttons on the machine. The look on his face makes me uneasy.

"What's wrong?" There's a long pause before he removes the probe and wipes the gel from my stomach. I push up to a sitting position. "Dr. Young?"

"I'm so sorry, Svetlana. Your baby doesn't have a heartbeat."

"What? No, that can't be." Tears well up in my eyes. "You need to look again."

"According to your dates and the results of the blood work, you should be at twelve, almost thirteen weeks gestation. But the fetus is measuring at what I'd expect for the beginning of the tenth week. There's no movement and no heartbeat."

I hear all his words, but they don't make sense. "What does that mean?"

"Your baby stopped developing about three weeks ago," he explains patiently. "I know from our phone calls that you were experiencing nausea and fatigue. Did those things happen to go away?"

"I've been feeling much better. Everything I read said that's normal for starting the second trimester."

"That's true, but a loss of pregnancy symptoms can also indicate early pregnancy loss. Have you had any cramping or spotting?"

"No, nothing." Which is why he has to be wrong.

"Sometimes a woman's body misses the cues that the baby is no longer growing."

"Can you fix it?"

"No, sweetheart. There's nothing I can do." Dr. Young takes my hand in his. "We need to talk about what happens next. Is there anyone you want to be here with you?"

"No." Brandon's the only person I want, and he's on the other side of the world. "What happens now?"

"Ordinarily, I'd offer you the choice of waiting for the miscarriage to happen naturally or offering a D&C. However, there's another issue that's of concern to me." When I don't speak, he continues. "The ultrasound showed that your placenta is at the top of your cervix and looks to be something called placenta accreta."

"What does that mean?"

"It's when the placenta grows too deeply into the uterine wall."

"Is that what caused this?" I can't say the word because then this will be real.

"No. This is a completely separate diagnosis. Unfortunately, we probably will never know the exact cause of the miscarriage."

I want to slap my hands over my ears and run like I did when Papa tried to tell me Jelena was gone, but I force myself to remain rooted in place.

"You're my last patient this afternoon. I'd prefer to take you to the operating room immediately for the D&C procedure."

"Can't it wait?"

"The longer we wait, the greater the chance for complications. It's much safer if I operate today," Dr. Young says. "I know how difficult this is. My wife and I lost our first baby, too." I nod as tears begin to fall. "Who can I call to be here with you?"

"Pyotr," I whisper and hand the doctor my phone with his contact pulled up.

He offers me a kind smile and presses the green call button. While the doctor explains what's going on to Pyotr, I lie down and curl into a ball on my side.

"He's on his way," he says softly. "Do you want me to stay with you until he comes?" I shake my head. "I'll send him back as soon as he gets here." The door opens and closes, leaving me alone.

My mind is a whirlwind of thoughts and emotions, a tumultuous mix that's hard to untangle. It's only been a few weeks, but I had so many dreams for my baby's future—everything Brandon and I would share and teach our child, the places we'd explore together.

I had this image of Brandon's face lighting up with joy when he came home, and I told him we were going to be parents. I can still vividly picture him cradling our tiny newborn in his arms, a look of tenderness on his face. We were going to be a family with so many possibilities for our future.

But now, in a matter of minutes, it's all slipped away. My hopes and dreams shattered, leaving nothing but an empty space within me. My chest aches as I attempt to wrap my head around the reality of what's happening.

This is my fault. This wouldn't have happened if I'd listened to Brandon and not pushed myself the past few months. Three weeks ago. That was right around Alex and Natalie's wedding, and it's when I started to feel better. A pang of guilt washes over me for mistaking it as something good, a progression of my pregnancy rather than the death of my baby.

Amidst the sadness and confusion, my thoughts drift to the impending procedure. Dr. Young seemed very concerned about the placenta accreta. Fear seeps into my thoughts as I grapple with the uncertainty of what lies ahead. Once again, I wish Brandon was here.

My fingers move to call him, but I freeze. There's no way to tell him that I was pregnant and never told him. I can't call him and tell him I've lost a baby he didn't know existed. As the room envelops me in silence, my mind fluctuates between the pain of loss and the longing for support. Pyotr will be here soon. I keep reminding myself. He'll help me get through this.

I don't know how long I lay here before the door opens, and Pyotr rushes to my side. "I'm here, little butterfly." As soon as I hear his voice, the dam breaks, and my heartache pours out. Pyotr scoops me into his arms and holds me close as I cry. "Did you call Brandon yet?"

"No." My voice quivers as I hold back a strangled sob.

"I'll call him." Pyotr reaches for his phone, but I grab his hand.

"You can't. He doesn't know."

"What do you mean?"

"I didn't tell him I was pregnant. Please don't call him."

"Lana, he should know." Pyotr gently urges me.

"Not like this. Not when he's so far away," I beg. "Please, Pyotr."

"Okay." He kisses my forehead. "We can wait."

The door cracks open, and Dr. Young returns. "You must be Pyotr?"

"I am."

"I'm sorry to meet under these circumstances. We're ready to take Lana up to pre-op."

"Can I stay with her?"

"Until she's ready to go into surgery, yes." Pyotr stands with me in his arms. "There's a wheelchair outside the door," Dr. Young says. Pyotr carefully lowers me into the chair and moves to the handles. Dr. Young walks with us and explains, "The procedure should take about thirty minutes," he explains. "I'll come and speak to you when I'm done. Then, when Svetlana's awake, they'll bring you to her."

"I need to be outside of whatever room she's in at all times."

"I'm afraid that's not possible in the surgery suite."

"This is non-negotiable. It's a matter of safety. You are familiar with Alexander Montgomery?" Pyotr asks, lowering his voice.

"I am."

"We work for the same employer. My presence is a requirement."

"I see. I'll make the necessary arrangements."

"Thank you."

When we arrive at the pre-op area, we're introduced to an older nurse. "This is Esperanza. She'll take over from here." Dr. Young places his hand on my shoulder. "I'm going to scrub in. I'll see you in the operating room."

"Right this way." The woman leads us to a small private room. "I need you to put this on." She hands me a hospital gown. "I'll be back in a few minutes."

Pyotr leaves my side only long enough for me to change.

"I'm scared, Pyotr."

"I know, butterfly." He sits next to me. "I'll be here the whole time."

"Excuse me," Esperanza says. "I know this is all happening quite quickly. Are there any questions you have?"

"This procedure," Pyotr says. "Is it safe?"

"A D&C is a standard procedure. As with any surgery, there

are risks, but overall, it's safe." Her voice is kind. "Svetlana's in good hands." She turns to me. "I'm going to get your IV started."

"Okay," I say with a shaky voice.

Esperanza places my IV with expertise and then prepares a syringe.

"What's that?" Pyotr asks, putting himself between the nurse and me.

"It's just a sedative," she explains. "Something to help Lana relax before the procedure."

I watch as she inserts the needle into the IV tubing. "Don't leave me, Pyotr." I cling to his hand.

"I'm right here, little butterfly." His voice sounds far away. "I'm not going anywhere."

Svetlana

〰

LIGHTS.

Smells.

Pain.

Beep. Beep. Beep.

Slowly, my eyes open. "Where am I?" My voice is gravelly.

I move to sit and groan in pain.

"Don't try to sit up yet," Pyotr says, placing his hand gently on my shoulder. "I'll call for the doctor now that you're awake."

"I'm so thirsty."

"Let me help you." He carefully lifts my head and holds a straw to my lips. "Just take a small sip, okay?"

The cold liquid soothes my sandpaper throat.

The door opens, allowing bright light from the hallway to creep into the dimly lit room. "She's awake?" Dr. Young asks quietly.

"She is." Pyotr gently lays my head on the pillow before setting the plastic cup on the bedside tray.

"Can you help me sit up?" Pyotr looks to Dr. Young, who nods before pushing the button that raises the head of my bed. I wince and wrap my arms around my abdomen and realize there's an incision. "I thought the procedure was done through my cervix?"

"We need to talk, butterfly," Pyotr says and sits on the edge of my bed.

Dr. Young pulls a chair closer and takes a seat. "Do you remember we discussed the placenta accreta I saw on the ultrasound?"

"Yes," I say hesitantly.

"When I got in there, it was worse than I anticipated. You had a rare condition called placenta percreta. Instead of the placenta being adhered too deeply in the uterine walls, it grew through them and attached to your bladder." The doctor pauses, giving me a moment to digest the information. "I called in a urology specialist to assist me in the surgery. While we were attempting to separate the two, your uterus ruptured, and you began hemorrhaging. I did everything I could to save your uterus, but we couldn't get the bleeding under control."

I cover my ears, desperately trying to block out the truth that threatens to suffocate me. "Stop," I plead, my voice trembling with anguish. "I don't want to hear anymore."

"Svetlana, please try to calm down." The doctor attempts to console me as if relaxation is possible in the wake of such devastation.

"Can you please leave us?" Pyotr asks, his voice laced with quiet authority.

"I think it's best I stay and explain to her—" Dr. Young attempts to argue, but Pyotr's unwavering stance demands compliance.

"I'm no longer asking." Pyotr stands. "You need to leave. I'll take care of her."

"Do you want me to order a sedative?" he asks as he stands.

"No." Pyotr turns back to me.

"I understand," the older man says softly. "I'll be back later to check on Lana. In the meantime, if you need anything, have me paged." He walks away with his shoulders hunched. As the door closes behind him, Pyotr moves closer, his presence a balm for my shattered soul.

I lower my hands, my vision blurred by tears. I meet his gaze, searching for solace amidst the wreckage of my hopes and dreams. "I can't have another baby, can I?" I ask, my voice choked with a pain that threatens to consume me.

"No, little butterfly. You can't," Pyotr replies, his voice filled with tenderness. Tears stream down my face. Each drop represents a piece of my irreparable loss. "They tried everything to stop the bleeding, but it came down to a hysterectomy or your life. Dr. Young rightfully chose your life."

The weight of his words crashes down on me, the finality of the decision forcing me to confront a reality I never expected to face.

A hysterectomy.

My ability to bear life was stolen by the ruthless hands of fate.

Bile rises in the back of my throat, and I begin retching and gasping for air, the agony of the truth leaving me breathless. My body's wracked with pain that mirrors the anguish in my heart.

Pyotr's arms envelop me, his embrace my lifeline in this storm. "Svetlana," he whispers, his voice thick with sorrow. "We need to call Brandon."

"No, Pyotr, please," I beg, my voice quivering with fear.

"He deserves to know. You need to allow him to grieve with you."

"I can't... I can't tell him. Brandon can't know."

Pyotr's hold on me tightens. "Butterfly, Brandon needs to be told."

I shake my head, my tears mixing with the ache in my heart. "No, Pyotr, you can't tell him." I look up, begging him to understand. "You have to promise me you won't say anything."

He softens his voice. "You know I'll support whatever decision you make."

Pyotr's been there for me since I was a little girl. Throughout my life, he's been my anchor when the storms rage around me.

Every trial I've endured, it's always been him I could run to, knowing he'd provide unwavering support. "I'm so scared, Pyotr," I whisper, my voice laced with vulnerability.

His touch is familiar, soothing. "No matter what happens, I'll always be here for you."

At that moment, with Pyotr's arms wrapped around me, I allow myself to grieve. To shatter in the arms of my bodyguard, knowing he'll be there to help me pick up the pieces.

Brandon

PER CHARLOTTE CLARKE'S ORDERS, WE ARRIVE AT THE Montgomery's early on Thanksgiving morning. When we walk into the apartment, everyone's already hard at work.

"There you are," Charlotte says when she sees Lana. "How are you feeling, sweetheart?" She goes to hug Lana, but Lana flinches away.

"I'm still sore but getting better every day." Lana forces a smile.

I stand back as the two ladies talk for a few minutes, wishing Lana's words were true. She hasn't been the same since I got back from Russia. At first, I thought it was that she still wasn't feeling well from the burst appendix or that maybe she was overly drowsy from the pain meds. She's no longer on pain meds, and nothing's improving. Lana's becoming more withdrawn every day.

Our conversation the other night about our contract convinced me that something serious is going on. She asked for things that were out of character for her. Things she knows I can never give her. The whole time, she acted as though our dynamic was nothing more than an annoyance, something she was trying to get rid of.

Desperate for answers, I texted Pyotr, but he said Lana seemed fine to him. I'm at a loss for what else to do.

"What do you think, Brandon?" Charlotte asks and motions to Lana, who's wearing her new apron.

"Wow." Lana stands beside Natalie's mom, covered in pumpkins and turkeys. "She's never looked more beautiful."

Lana rolls her eyes, a move that would get her ass smacked if she wasn't still recovering.

"I told you he'd love it." Charlotte turns and grabs a glass baking dish filled with sweet potatoes. "Brandon, come and take this for her. You two are going to make my famous sweet potato casserole." She hands Lana a note card. "Here's the recipe. Everything's in the tray."

Svetlana looks down at the card in her hand. Charlotte looks between us, seemingly as confused by Lana's silence as I am.

"We'll get right on it," I say and give Charlotte a big smile.

"If you get stuck, let me know."

We find an empty spot at the kitchen island. I set the baking dish down and pull out one of the tall stools for Lana to sit. "Are you comfortable? I can get a pillow for your back."

"I'm okay." Lana's answer is quiet.

"Are you going to join us or just keep watching?" Charlotte asks, and I turn around to see Natalie standing outside the kitchen.

"I was just watching everyone together." She walks over and puts her arm around her mom. "You have no idea how happy this makes me."

"I think I do, sweetheart. Alex was kind enough to buy breakfast for everyone. Grab yourself a bagel, and then get over there and help your husband set the table."

On her way to get breakfast, Natalie comes over to Lana. "I'm so glad to see you. Brandon said you weren't feeling well. I was afraid you weren't going to make it today."

"I'm fine." Lana doesn't look up from peeling her potato.

Natalie glances at me, and I shrug. I was hopeful being around everyone would pull her out of whatever funk she's been in, but so far, that isn't happening. Which worries me even more.

Several hours later, everyone's gathered around Alex and Natalie's dining room table that's overflowing with a plethora of steaming dishes.

"Before we eat, we always go around the table and say something we're thankful for," Stanley says. "I'll start. I'm thankful to be here, in this crazy city, celebrating with my daughter and son-in-law."

"This is the first time I'm celebrating an American Thanksgiving," Amelia says, beaming. "I'm thankful for being safe, for having food to eat." She looks at Max and Irina. "And for having a new family."

"Our family has much to be thankful for," Maxim adds. "Amelia's adoption was finalized last week. She is now legally Amelia Solonik, our daughter." He smiles proudly.

"You didn't tell me the adoption was finalized," I whisper to Lana.

"I didn't? It must have slipped my mind."

Slipped her mind? I'm puzzled by her odd answer. Lana was so ecstatic about having a little sister. I don't buy that the finalizing of Amelia's adoption slipped her mind, but now's not the time to get into it.

"I'm thankful that Svetlana is on the road to recovery after her surgery scare," I say when it's my turn.

"I second that," Natalie says, smiling at her best friend.

"I'm thankful for that, too," Lana says quickly.

Alex goes next. "This amazing woman sitting beside me has made me the happiest man in the world. She's given me so much more than I ever thought I'd have. Thankful doesn't come close to expressing my feelings today." He leans over to kiss his wife. They exchange quiet whispers.

Stanley clears his throat. "Let's hold hands and say grace."

I haven't had a big family Thanksgiving since my parents passed away. Being here with my new family is wonderful but bittersweet at the same time. I wish my own Mom and Dad were here. They would've loved Lana as much as I do. And maybe Mom would've been able to give me advice on what to do about the distance that's growing between us.

Svetlana

After dinner, Natalie goes downstairs with Viktor while we transform the apartment for Natalie's baby shower. It's the one part of the day I've been dreading since Charlotte called and asked for my help.

My phone rings, and I see Charlotte Clarke's name pop up. She's never called me before.

"Hello?"

"Svetlana? It's Charlotte, Natalie's mom."

"How are you?"

"I'm doing well. Natalie told me about your health scare. I hope you're on the mend."

"I'm getting a little better every day," I tell a half-truth. Physically, I'm recovering, but emotionally, the pain only grows worse.

"I'm glad to hear that. Listen, I have a favor to ask."

"What is it?"

"I want to throw a baby shower for Natalie while we're in town. I'm thinking after Thanksgiving dinner," she says. "It won't be as lavish as one of Alexander's surprise affairs, but it'll be lovely nonetheless."

"I'm sure Natalie will love that."

"I know you're still recovering," she says hesitantly, "But you

and Natalie are so close, I don't want to leave you out of the planning."

"Thank you for thinking of me, but you're right. I'm not really up to doing much."

"As long as you're going to be there. That's the most important."

"I'll be there."

"You look exhausted," Alex says, coming over to where I'm standing out of the way watching.

"I am."

"Charlotte and Irina have everything under control here. Why don't you go lie down while they get everything ready? I'll send Brandon to wake you up before we start."

"That is a good idea, *moya babochka*," Papa adds. "You are too pale."

"I'm just tired, Papa. I think I'll take Alex up on his suggestion and take a short nap."

"You can use the bed in the room Mama and I are staying in."

"Thank you." I kiss his cheek.

"Svetlana." An unfamiliar voice calls my name and gently shakes my shoulder. "Svetlana, it's time to wake up."

I open my eyes and see Amelia looking over me.

"It's time for the baby shower," she says with a big smile.

I push myself up and flinch. My stomach still hurts when I try to use the muscles.

"Do you need help?" She offers her hand.

"No, thank you."

Amelia looks toward the door. "I'll leave you alone."

"Amelia, wait," I say, reaching out for her hand and making her jump.

"I'm sorry. You startled me."

"I shouldn't have grabbed at you." I give her a small smile. "I wanted to apologize for not coming home for your adoption."

I'd grown to love the video chats Amelia and I had every night. She's sixteen and mature beyond her years in some respects, but in others, she's still a little girl. We spent hours pouring over virtual paint samples and décor to redecorate her new room and planned all the things we were going to do together when I came home to visit. But that hasn't happened.

"You don't have to do that. You're recovering."

"I know, but I should've been there. Can you keep a secret?" She nods. "I'm flying home with you guys after Thanksgiving. I'm planning to stay for a while, so we'll be able to get to know each other."

It's an idea I came up with while I showered this morning. Things between Brandon and I are tense, too tense. He's accepted my excuse of recovering. But I know it's wearing thin. He's going to start asking questions. Ones I can't answer. Going home for a while will give me the space I desperately need to clear my head and think. To figure out what to do next.

"Really? That'll be so much fun. Is Brandon coming with you?"

"No," I say sadly. "He has to stay here to work. He doesn't know yet, so please don't say anything."

"You have my word." She pretends to zip her lips and throw away the key.

I put a fake smile on my face. "We better get out there before we miss all the fun."

When I step out of the hallway into the main living area, I gasp. Star, Anthony, and Leo have arrived for the shower. The apartment is now bathed in pink and elephants.

"How did you do all this?" Natalie asks as she steps off the elevator with Viktor.

"Your mother's a very efficient party planner," Mama says.

"I've missed seeing you." Star gives Natalie a big hug.

"Look at you, girl." Leo rubs her tummy. "How's my little niece?"

"She's very active today."

"I feel that." He laughs.

"You look terrific, Natalie." Tony hugs her. "Pregnancy suits you."

This hurts so damn much. I love my best friend, but I can't stop the pain and resentment festering inside, seeing how happy everyone is for Natalie. Brandon and I were supposed to be engaged right now. He was supposed to be standing proudly by my side, like Alex is with Natalie, knowing he was going to be a father. Natalie and I would be pregnant together. Maybe we'd be sharing this baby shower? But now all that's gone.

"Let's have dessert, shall we?" Alex leads Natalie to the table, and we all take our seats.

Charlotte, Mama, and Amelia carry in pies and a two-tiered pink and grey baby cake.

"Look at that cake," Natalie squeals. "It's adorable. How did you manage to get this on a holiday?"

"I told you Maxim is bossy," Charlotte chuckles. "He's responsible for that."

"Thank you so much, *dedushka*."

"Nothing will stop me from giving you and *moya vnuchka* everything."

His words are like a punch to the gut. He's my baby's *dedushka*—was. I'm reminded that Papa will never have a biological grandchild.

"Mrs. Clarke. You must give me your recipe for this pecan pie. My customers will love it," Tony gushes.

"You want to use my recipe for your restaurant?"

"Of course, I'll compensate you for it."

"There's no need for that, Anthony." Charlotte waves her hand at him. "I'd be honored for you to have it."

I pick at a piece of pumpkin pie while everyone else chatters about all things baby. I do my best to smile when I'm supposed to and pretend I'm having a good time. I'm struggling with self-hatred, but I don't want to ruin today for Natalie. This will probably be the last time I see her, so I take a deep breath and, with as much cheerfulness as I can muster, say, "Let's get to the presents."

"That sounds like a great idea. I can't wait to open them." Natalie returns my smile.

Alex helps Natalie get comfortable in an armchair next to the stack of presents. Charlotte had already asked me to help with the gifts. Carefully, I cut the ribbons from each package and pass them to Amelia. Charlotte said something about making a hat that Natalie has to wear. I think it's bizarre, but I do as I've been instructed.

"Oh, Mom. It's stunning." Natalie holds up a baby quilt with elephants on it.

"The ladies from church worked on it with me. I was hoping you'd like it."

"I don't just like it. I love it."

"It's exquisite, Charlotte," Alex says as he inspects the stitching. "This was truly a labor of love, and we'll cherish it."

Next are Brandon and my gifts. She opens the first one, a designer baby pram. It's the same one I have on my secret Pinterest board.

"I read it's all the rage with high society in the city," I say, waving my hand.

"It's stunning," Natalie says.

Our other gift is something else from *my* wish list. It's a bassinet that rocks in different patterns and can mimic how a mama rocks their baby. My heart aches.

"The lady at the store said this thing is magic," Brandon adds and shrugs.

"It's a smart bassinet," Alex says as he reads the box. "It'll sense if the baby is fussing and gently rock her."

"I figured if it works, I'll get the award for best uncle."

Everyone shares a laugh. I smile and pretend all the while I'm dying inside.

I've been passing gifts for what feels like forever, but finally, we get to the last one. Beautiful hand-painted pictures for the nursery wall.

"Thank you all so very much. This is more than we could've asked for," Natalie says, wiping the tears from her eyes.

"You've made today extra special for my family." Alex lovingly caresses Natalie's tummy. "Thank you all so much."

"We're not done yet," Charlotte says and stands with a mound of ribbons.

While they do whatever they're doing, I excuse myself before I lose it in front of everyone. Quietly, I slip back into the room my parents are staying in and sit on the bed.

Several minutes later, there's a knock on the door. I stay quiet, hoping whoever it is goes away. Instead, the door opens, and Natalie peeks in, "Do you mind some company?"

"It's fine. Just close the door, please."

She sits next to me. "Are you going to tell me what's going on?"

I turn my head, not wanting to have this conversation but knowing there's no way to avoid it. "Things aren't okay between Brandon and me."

"I know."

"Is it that obvious?"

"To me, yes. What's going on?"

"He wants more," I say, pulling my legs onto the bed.

"What's wrong with that?"

"I don't."

Lies. I'm burying myself in so many lies.

"What do you mean you don't? I thought you loved him?" she asks, clearly confused.

"He's a great Dominant, and I care about him." I do my best to sound flippant.

"I sense a but coming."

"He's ready to settle down. He wants what you and Alex have

—the husband/wife thing." I wave my hand and sigh loudly. "He wants to be a father."

"And what do you want?" she asks softly.

"I love the club and public scenes. I might want to try adding other people." Natalie's eyes go wide. "I'm not ready for marriage, and having kids isn't possible." I stop quickly, realizing what I just said and hoping she doesn't catch on.

"Have you talked to him? Told him how you're feeling?"

"I told him what I want and what I don't want. We've been trying to renegotiate our contract but haven't reached any agreements."

"What does that mean?" I hear the worry in her tone.

"We're not on the same page anymore. So, we're putting our dynamic on hold." Pain grips my insides, tearing me apart.

"Don't do anything you'll regret. Give it some more time. Keep trying to work it out."

The door opens, and Brandon steps in. "There you two are. Alex is looking for you, Nat."

Natalie squeezes my hand. "Please give what I said some thought."

I nod but say nothing for fear if I do, everything I'm hiding will spill out, and the fractured pieces I'm barely holding together will shatter, and I'll never recover.

Svetlana

"Good morning, sleepyhead," Brandon says when I walk into the kitchen. "I made breakfast." He places a soft kiss against my lips. "Sit down, and I'll make your plate."

I pull out a chair and quietly sit as Brandon puts scrambled eggs and toast on my plate.

"Here you go."

"Thank you." I pick up my fork and take a small bite.

"How do you feel today?"

"Okay." I shrug and play with the food on my plate.

Brandon's eyes search mine. Worry is etched across his face. "I don't understand why Pyotr didn't call me.

"You and Papa were busy," I reply, my voice softening. "I didn't want to worry you unnecessarily."

"You come first," Brandon says, his voice filled with sincerity, as he cups my cheek tenderly. "Always."

His touch sends a shiver down my spine, and I feel the weight of my guilt pressing upon me. My heart aches as he leans in and kisses me, a gesture filled with affection. Affection I don't deserve.

As our lips part, a heavy silence hangs in the air. I intended to tell Brandon the truth when he got home, but then he told me about the child trafficking ring. He was still devastated, knowing two children died during the shootout. When Brandon expressed his hope that the work Papa and his network of heroes do today will make the world a better place for our future children, I knew I couldn't do it.

I made a split-second decision to tell him I had an emergency appendectomy. It was wrong, I know. It's a lie I'll never be able to come back from—I'm aware of that, too. But what's done is done. Nothing good lasts forever.

"Alex called this morning," Brandon says, a smile playing on his face. "He's invited everyone to their house for Thanksgiving next week."

"Who's everyone?"

"His dad and Luna. Max, Irina, and Amelia." He pauses. "And Stanley and Charlotte."

"All at the same time?"

"That's how the holiday works," Brandon chuckles nervously, trying to disperse some of the tension. "They want us to come over for Pie Day, too. I told him we'll be there."

A mix of joy and dread washes over me. Joy because I love spending time with our families, and dread because I know my guilt will only intensify in their presence.

Brandon reaches out and takes my hand. "What's wrong, *papillon*?" he asks softly, his voice laced with concern.

I take another deep breath, gathering my thoughts. Once again, the truth sits on the tip of my tongue. If I tell it now, I can mitigate the damage. But if I tell him I'm unable to carry his child, he'll stay with me out of pity and his sense of honor. Brandon will never have the child he's always wanted. I search for the strength to speak the words that have been haunting me, but it's not there. I'm too weak. "I don't know if I'll be up to going out two days in a row." The lie drips from my lips, and I lose what little appetite I have.

"I didn't even think about that. I can call and cancel."

"No, don't do that." I might not have grown up celebrating Thanksgiving, but I know it's an important celebration here. One that revolves around gathering with family and friends. It's a holiday Brandon loves. I refuse to take this away from him. "If you don't mind, maybe I'll stay home from Pie Day so I have the energy to go on Thanksgiving."

"Whatever you need to do while you're recovering." He looks at the nearly full plate I've pushed away. "You've barely touched your breakfast."

"I'm not hungry," I mutter, my voice low and lacking in energy.

"Go lie down. I'll do the dishes, then come up, and we can watch a movie," he suggests, his tone gentle but carrying a sense of determination.

"Actually, we need to talk," I interject, my voice sounding weary.

"About our engagement?" he asks hopefully, his tone rising slightly.

"That and our contract," I confirm, my voice heavy with the weight of the conversation.

"Oh yeah. I almost forgot about that," he replies casually, his tone not fully grasping the seriousness of the situation.

When we originally signed our contract, I requested that we set a date to renegotiate. I almost didn't ask, but given the circumstances now, I'm glad I did.

"Are you sure you're up to that?" Brandon asks with genuine concern.

"I am."

"Okay. I'll be up in a few minutes."

While I wait for Brandon, I find myself rehearsing my words repeatedly. I know he won't take it well, but I have to do something to start putting some space between us.

"I grabbed a copy of the contract," Brandon says, waving the papers in his hand. "Are you sure you want to do this now?"

"Yes."
Brandon, I'm so sorry for what I'm about to do.

Svetlana

"WHAT THE HELL DO YOU MEAN YOU'RE GOING BACK TO Russia?" Brandon yells as I'm packing.

"I want to spend some time with Amelia. Get to know my new sister," I say while trying to fold a shirt. My hands are shaking so badly that the task is impossible, so I ball it up and toss it into the suitcase.

"What about the bar exam?" he asks.

"I'll reschedule it for another time." I throw more clothes in.

"What about us?" Brandon asks quietly.

I freeze and look into his stormy grey eyes. Eyes that I'm going to miss so damn much. "I think the distance will do us some good while we figure everything out."

"You're fucking kidding, right? The last thing we need is distance."

"I'm not kidding. We—" I motion between us. "We need some space. Time to figure out what we want."

"I thought we already knew what we wanted." Brandon grabs my arms, holding me tight. "What's going on with you, *papillon*?"

"What do you mean?"

"First, you didn't call me to tell me you were sick or to let me know you were having surgery. You haven't been the same since I got back from Russia." His eyes plead with me to confide in him. "And now you tell me you're leaving me."

"I feel like I'm drowning. There's too much on my plate," I say quickly. "I need to take a step back. I need to go home."

"I'll go with you." He turns to go to the closet, undoubtedly to grab his suitcase.

"No," I say, and he stops moving. "Alex is giving you his company. You can't just walk away from that."

"How long are you going to be gone?"

"I don't know."

"What can I do to get you to change your mind?" he asks, desperation written all over him.

"Please don't make this any harder than it already is." I close my suitcase, lock it, and drag it off the bed. "I need to do this for me. Please try to understand."

"I'd love to understand, but how do you expect me to do that if you won't talk to me? If you refuse to tell me what's really happening."

"I told you why. I want to get to know—"

"Yes. I know. You want to get to know Amelia." He throws his hands up. "But I also know that's not the truth. That's nothing more than your excuse for whatever's really going on."

My phone buzzes.

Pyotr: Maxim's outside. Are you ready to go?

Me: I'll be down in a minute.

"You're really leaving." Brandon's shoulders sag in defeat.

"I have to," I say sadly.

He grabs the handle of my suitcase and storms out of the room. I follow a few steps behind, watching him walk down the steps and head straight for the door. Wordlessly, he passes Pyotr, who's waiting for me in the foyer.

"I take it you didn't tell him?" I shake my head. "Svetlana..."

I can count on one hand the times Pyotr referred to me by my given name. None of them were good. "This is hard enough as it is. Please don't start on me, too."

"This wouldn't be nearly as hard if you'd tell him the truth."

"Your bag is in the car," Brandon says, interrupting us. "I take it you're not going to tell me what the hell's going on either." He glares at Pyotr.

"I'm sorry," Pyotr says softly. "I'll be outside."

When Brandon looks at me, the betrayal in his eyes nearly brings me to my knees. This mess is all my fault, and although leaving is tearing me in two, it's the best option. The hurt Brandon's experiencing by my leaving is nothing compared to what he'd feel knowing I lost our baby and kept it from him. That I can never give him the child he wants.

Once I'm gone, he'll heal. He'll move on and be happy with someone else.

"Please, Svetlana. I'm begging you not to do this."

I reach out and cup his cheek. "I love you, Brandon." My lips touch his for the briefest of seconds before I hurry from the house.

Brandon

My hand shoots out, grabbing the doorframe as I watch the woman who's my world slide into the back seat of her father's rented car. The door closes, and they drive away. I watch until the vehicle is out of sight.

How am I supposed to go on without her here? Why does it feel like she was saying goodbye—for good? Tears flow in rivulets down my face, and my lungs struggle for my next breath.

I close my door and drag myself to the living room, where I drop onto the sofa. Nothing makes sense right now.

It's been days since I went to work. I don't know when I ate last. I'm still in the clothes I was wearing when Svetlana left me. Nothing in my world is right.

I'm drifting in and out of a restless sleep when my cell rings. I don't bother looking at the screen.

"Hello?"

"Brandon?" Viktor asks.

"Yeah."

"I don't know how to tell you this."

"Tell me what?" I sit up. What else can possibly go wrong?

"It's Alex." Viktor's voice cracks. "He's dead."

Everything that happened with Svetlana has my head screwed up to the point that I'm hallucinating. "Can you repeat that, please?"

"There was an explosion at the new building. Alex didn't make it out." I hold the phone to my ear but don't say anything. I can't. There's no way this is really happening. "Brandon? Are you there?"

"I'm here. What the hell happened?" I listen carefully as Viktor explains that Alex was getting into his car in the parking garage when the car exploded with him in it. "Who's behind it?"

"I don't know. I don't fucking know," Viktor says, his voice full of pain.

Natalie. Oh my God. She's just recovered after their ordeal in Mexico. Now this. "Are Natalie and the baby okay?" I ask as I drag myself off the couch. I need to take a shower and find some clean clothes. I have to get over there.

"She's devastated."

"Give me an hour, and I'll be there." I hang up and take the steps two at a time. Without thinking, I bring up Svetlana's contact and hit the green call button. Her voicemail picks up. "Lana, I need to talk to you. It's important. Please call me."

I don't wait for her to return my call. I turn the hot water on and allow the steam to fill the bathroom, clouding my reflection in the mirror. After I shed my clothes, I step under the hot spray. The water cascades over me, soothing my weary body but failing to wash away the chaos within. Thoughts of Svetlana, Alex, and Natalie swirl in my mind, mingling with regret, grief, and a desperate longing for things to be different.

The water pounds against my skin, almost as if trying to wake me from this nightmare. But reality is just as harsh and unforgiving. Alex, my best friend, is gone. Ripped away from everyone who cares about him in an explosion that's been made to look like a tragic accident. Even without all the details, I'm certain that's not the truth. Someone is behind this. The shock of his loss shakes me to the core, a reminder of the fragility of life and the pain that often accompanies it.

With trembling hands, I turn off the shower and step out, wrapping a towel around my waist. Water drips from my hair, mingling with the tears I've been holding back for too long. I glance at myself in the mirror, seeing the reflection of a broken man, haunted by his past and uncertain of his future.

I dry myself off quickly and put on fresh clothes. Right now, my mind is fixated on one thing—being there for Natalie. She's pregnant and has just lost her husband. I can't imagine the depth of her sorrow. Despite my own struggles, I have to be strong for her, for both of us.

As I reach for my phone to check the time, I notice a missed text.

Svetlana: Papa told me.

I call her back, hoping against hope that she'll answer. My heart sinks when her voicemail picks up again, but I don't leave another message. As much as I need to hear her voice, it's clear she doesn't want to speak to me. My hands shake as I put down the phone and take a deep breath, trying to steady myself. The weight of the world rests on my shoulders, but there's no time for self-pity. Natalie's going to need all of us to get through the horrific tragedy.

As I drive toward Alex and Natalie's house, rain begins to fall, adding to the somberness of the day. The windshield wipers move rhythmically. Their sound doing nothing to drown out the thoughts rapidly running through my mind.

While I navigate the congested New York City streets, I do my best to put aside my own heartache and prepare to be the pillar of strength Natalie's going to need. I'll be by her side as we find a way to navigate the storm that has engulfed our lives.

Brandon

"WHERE IS SHE?" I ASK AS THE ELEVATOR DOORS OPEN, and I burst out.

"Excuse me." Charlotte Clarke appears in the foyer with her hands on her hips. "May I ask what you think you're doing?"

"I'm sorry, Mrs. Clarke." I take a deep breath, trying to remember they've all just experienced an unexpected loss. "Viktor called and told me what happened. I'm here to see Natalie."

"The doctor said she needs to rest."

"I understand. I just—"

"Brandon," Viktor interrupts our exchange. In an uncharacteristic move, he steps around Charlotte and embraces me. "I'm so sorry."

"I was hoping to get here, and it would be a bad joke," I say, clearing my throat.

Charlotte quietly excuses herself.

"I still can't believe it's real." Viktor quickly wipes his eyes.

"Have you heard anything yet?" I ask, lowering my voice.

"Maxim's been apprised of the situation. He has Dimitri working all the angles, but there's been no information so far."

"Where's Natalie?"

"She's in the kitchen. Her mom's trying to get her to eat."

I follow Viktor and find Natalie sitting at the kitchen table, a bowl of soup in front of her. Instead of eating, she's playing with the spoon, circling it in the broth. Natalie doesn't look up when we step into the room. It's as if she's lost in her own little world. She's so pale, her skin is almost translucent, and her eyes are red-rimmed and swollen.

"I'm pretty sure she's in shock," Viktor whispers. "Dr. Young was here to check on her and the baby. He said they're doing okay but wants her to rest as much as possible."

"When is she going to catch a break?"

"Brandon?" Natalie's voice is barely audible.

"I'm here, sweetheart." I hurry over and wrap my arms around her. She slumps against me and begins to cry. "I've got you, Nat," I murmur repeatedly until her weeping subsides. Viktor slides a chair over for me, and I settle in beside her. "You should try to eat some."

"I'm not hungry."

"I know, but you have to think about the baby." I push the bowl to her. "You can do it. Just a few spoonfuls."

Natalie picks up the spoon and sips some broth from it. "Does Lana know?"

"She does. Maxim told her."

"Is she coming home?"

"I don't think so."

"What happened?" Natalie asks as a lone tear slides down her cheek. I wipe it with my thumb. "She told me you guys needed a break, and she was going home for a while."

"You know as much as I do." I sigh. "We were renegotiating our contract like we'd agreed when she blindsided me with all kinds of crazy requests." I guide her hand back to her bowl, hoping she'll take another spoonful of soup.

"I'll try to talk to her," Natalie offers.

"Thank you, but right now, you need to focus on yourself and the baby."

"I don't know how to do any of this without him," she says,

her eyes filling with tears once again. "Alex was my world. He was the other part of my heart, and now he's gone."

"I'm here, and Viktor's here." I rub her back and exchange a worried glance with Viktor. "We'll be by your side for every step. You won't have to do this on your own."

Even as I say the words, I know we have big shoes to fill. Alex is a good man—*was* a good man. He always put himself and his needs behind those of others. Not only did he run a successful company, but he was also about to open a treatment center for rescued victims of human trafficking. As a husband, he treasured Natalie, and I know he would've been an incredible father to baby Rose. No one will ever replace him, but I'll do everything in my power to be sure Rose knows exactly who her father was and that Natalie will never be alone.

We aren't family by blood but family by choice. Somehow, we'll take the pieces of our fractured lives and learn how to live again.

Svetlana

"Natalie's your best friend. Her husband was just killed. She's going to need everyone who cares about her to get through this," Mama reprimands me. "I don't understand how you can refuse to fly back with us."

"I just can't." I walk away and turn toward the window, unable to face her.

At first, I didn't believe Papa when he told me Alex had been killed. I couldn't imagine why he would joke about something so awful. It wasn't a joke, though. Once the initial shock wore off, I found myself struggling to wrap my head around the fact that Alex was dead.

I've been in Papa's world long enough to know that things like car explosions usually aren't an accident. Someone set out to kill him. Papa has all his men working the case. Whoever did this can run, but they can't hide. Papa will find the responsible people, and he'll make them pay.

"I don't understand what's going on with you, Svetlana." Mama comes to stand next to me. Softening her voice, she says, "Please help me to understand."

"There's nothing to understand. I came home to spend time

with Amelia. She's devastated about what happened. I'm not going to leave her here alone."

When Mama told Amelia about the explosion and that Alex was gone, she fell apart. She couldn't understand why someone would want to hurt him. We were concerned it would set back her recovery, but right now, she seems to be holding her own. She only asked if Papa would find out who did it and take care of them.

Papa didn't want Amelia to know what he did outside of Jelena's Hope. When they were getting ready to enroll her in school, I suggested he tell her. She would hear it from the kids at school, which would've been more of a shock than Papa telling her. Amelia is very perceptive, and I suspect she already has an idea. Either way, it seemed to help her feel more secure both at home and with Papa.

They asked if she wanted to go to New York with them, but she said no. She didn't think she could handle attending the funeral.

My parents left yesterday. It'll be a quick trip to New York for the funeral and back home. Papa has been very hands-on with searching for who's behind the explosion. I haven't seen him this distraught since Jelena was taken.

This evening is Alex's memorial service. Natalie and I have been on a video call for the past two hours. She's spent most of the time going from tears to silence. I assure her she doesn't have to talk but that I'll be here if she wants to.

"I don't know how I'm going to get through tonight," Natalie says as she tries to do her make-up. "How do I say goodbye to him?"

"I hate that I'm not there with you." Fate has been cruel lately.

We've both lost people who we loved very much. One a husband and soon-to-be-father and one an innocent baby who didn't get the chance to be born.

"I wish you were here too." Natalie sets her make-up brush down as a fresh wave of tears falls. "I don't think I can do this, Lana."

"I know this is hard, honey." I move the camera closer. "But you have to be strong. For Alex."

My words are weak. If she only knew what a cowardly hypocrite I am right now. I'm preaching to her to be strong while she's facing life without her husband. In comparison, my loss was nothing, and instead of being strong, I lied and ran.

In the background, Natalie's bedroom door opens, and Charlotte steps into the room. "Sam and Luna just got here. He'd like to see you."

"You can send him in." Natalie turns back to the camera. "I have to go. We'll talk soon?"

"I don't care what time it is. If you need me, just call. I love you, Nat."

"Love you too, Lan."

The screen goes black, and I break down. Just a few months ago, everything was perfect. Our best friends were married and getting ready to welcome their first baby. Brandon and I were about to announce our engagement, and I would surprise him with the news of our pregnancy. And now, we're here. Alex is dead. Natalie is a young widow who's facing giving birth and raising a child on her own. Our baby is gone, and Brandon and I are no longer together.

I want to stomp my feet and scream at just how unfair life is. But what good will that do? It won't bring back what we lost.

"Svetlana?" Amelia says my name, startling me.

I swipe at the wetness on my face and turn around. "What's up?"

"I heard you crying and wanted to be sure you're okay." Her voice is small and quiet.

"I'm good," I say, hoping she accepts my answer, but she doesn't.

"You don't have to hide your sadness from me," Amelia says, coming closer. "I won't break if you tell me the truth."

"I was just talking to Natalie." I pat the couch, inviting Amelia to join me. "She's getting ready for the memorial service."

Amelia sits and tucks her legs up under her. "Is she doing alright?"

"Not really. But Natalie's strong. She'll get through this."

"I should've gone with Max and Irina," she says, and her lip quivers. "Natalie's my friend. She's probably going to hate me now."

"Natalie would never hate you. She understands that you're still getting adjusted. When you're ready, you can call and talk to her."

"Are you sure she isn't going to be mad?"

"I'm positive." I smile at the girl—my sister. "What do you say we get dressed and go out for some dinner?"

It may seem callous to go out and do something fun while Natalie is going through hell, but I'm trying to think of Amelia. She's struggling in so many ways. The last thing she needs to worry about is whether Natalie will be mad at her or not. The only thing I can think of doing is trying to distract her.

"Um." She looks uncertain, and I think she's about to say no, but she surprises me by asking, "Will Pyotr be coming too?"

"He will, but he'll stay out of our way."

"But he'll be there, right?"

"Yes. Would it help if I asked Timur to come, too?"

"It would."

"How long will it take you to get ready?" I ask.

"Ten minutes." The corners of her mouth tip up in a small smile.

"Perfect." I smile.

We go our separate ways to change. Then, I search for the guys to let them know we're going out.

Brandon

THE SUN IS BEGINNING TO SET AS I ARRIVE AT THE stone chapel for Alex's memorial service. I left early, ensuring I was the first to arrive. I wanted the opportunity to say a few words to him before anyone else got here.

Stepping inside, I find the room lit by hundreds of flickering candles. The urn holding Alex's remains sits on a table beside a picture of Natalie and him holding one of the baby's ultrasound photos in front of her round tummy.

We were just together a few days ago for Natalie's shower. Alex was alive. There was so much to look forward to. Everyone was happy. I've reached for my phone to call him so many times over the past few days only to remind myself that he's gone.

"Max will search every corner of the earth to find whoever did this. Your death will not go unpunished." I swallow over the lump in my throat. "Don't worry about Natalie and the baby. I'll be there for her."

A hand lands on my shoulder. "You are a good friend, Brandon," Maxim says.

I drop my head. "We have to find who did this."

"We will," Maxim assures me. "Whoever is responsible will answer directly to me." I nod, satisfied with Maxim's response.

"Natalie and Viktor are pulling in now. I thought you would want to be with them."

"Thanks, Max." I turn and start walking away.

"Brandon," Max calls, and I turn to face him. "Everything will work out with Svetlana as well."

Hearing her name is painful. I wish she was here, by my side, helping me say goodbye to my best friend. I can't speak. My emotions are running too high. So, I say nothing and continue making my way to Natalie.

I find her standing next to Viktor, who's on high alert, as they greet the mourners who've come to pay their final respects.

"Is there anything you need?" I ask as I put my hand on Natalie's elbow.

"No, thank you."

"I'll be inside."

Maxim motions for me to sit by him and Irina. It's hard to be with them. It makes Lana's absence all the more painful, a void that deepens in their presence.

Alex should be here. He'd know what to do. He and Svetlana were close. If there was anyone who could get her to talk, to open up, it would be him. Instead, we're all here floundering without him and preparing to say our final goodbyes to a man none of us are ready to let go of.

Although we're in a chapel, the ceremony is not being led by a member of the clergy. Alex wasn't a fan of organized religion. Instead, Natalie asked me to deliver the eulogy. When she and Viktor take their seats, I rise and walk to the front of the room, unsure how to get through the words I wrote.

"Today, we gather to remember and honor a dear friend who left us too soon. We're all shocked and heartbroken by the suddenness of Alex's passing. Alex was a wonderful person who impacted the lives of all those he encountered. He had a unique ability to bring joy and laughter to any situation. Many of you know I dated Natalie's college roommate. Little did she know her arrival home one night would mark the beginning of an unforgettable tale. Natalie and I hadn't had the privilege of meeting one another yet. Actually, I don't think she knew I existed until late one night when she mistook me for an intruder. Natalie, armed with her cell phone flashlight, promptly declared that the NYPD was en route."

Laughter erupts, relieving some of the heaviness in the air.

"Thankfully, we were able to clear up the misunderstanding, sparing me a close encounter with handcuffs." It's a story that became a cherished part of our shared history and one we recount with endless amusement. "A year later, with a spark of inspiration, Svetlana and I orchestrated a blind date between Alex and Natalie. We didn't know that we were setting the stage for a love story that would forever be etched in our hearts."

I look at Natalie, who's wiping tears from her face and am reminded of the incredible journey she and Alex embarked on. Alex's presence in Natalie's life brought love, happiness, and countless cherished memories. They shared laughter, tears, and unwavering support for one another. Together, they wove a tapestry of love that will forever endure.

"Though we mourn our shared loss, we must also be grateful for the unforgettable chapters Alex authored in our lives. Alex's kindness knew no bounds, and although he's no longer with us, we can take comfort in knowing he's left a lasting impact on our lives. His spirit will continue to live on through the love he shared, the laughter he gifted us, and the immeasurable impact he made on our hearts. As we say our final goodbyes, I ask everyone to honor Alex's memory by embracing the love and laughter he so effortlessly brought into our lives. May his legacy serve as a reminder that the bonds we form and the moments we share are precious treasures to be cherished."

My voice cracks as the emotions I've been holding back break free. Tears fall unbidden as I look up and speak directly to the man whose untimely departure has left an undeniable void in my life. "I always admired you, Alex. Until we meet again, brother."

I step off the platform and walk over to Natalie, taking her trembling hand in mine. "You were his world, Natalie. Thank you for loving him." Her shoulders shudder as sobs wrack her body. I wrap my arms around her, hoping to offer her even a small measure of comfort.

How do we do this? Where the hell do we go from here?

Svetlana

"Svetlana," Papa calls as he rushes into the indoor swimming pool room. "Natalia is in labor."

"She's early," I say as I climb out of the pool.

"That is all you have to say?"

I wrap the towel around my dripping body. "I'm sure Viktor's with her."

"But Alexander is not."

Crossing my arms over my chest, I stare at Papa, neither of us backing down. I want to tell him everything. Open up about my heartache and loss, but I can't force the words to come out. The emotions remain locked deep inside. "People die. It's a part of life."

Papa takes a step closer. His presence is imposing, and I drop my arms. "When did you become so cold-hearted?" he asks, narrowing his eyes.

"I'm not cold-hearted, just realistic." I grab my bathing suit cover. "I need to get to the center. I'm volunteering there today."

"You will be well served to remember why Jelena's Hope was started."

I ignore Papa's last statement and hurry away.

As soon as I get inside the safety of my bedroom, the tears I was struggling to hold back can no longer be contained. I slide down the door and pull my knees up to my chest. The last time I spoke to Natalie was before Alex's memorial service. She's texted me several times, sending me ultrasound pictures and recordings of the baby's heartbeat. Each time I open one, my heart shatters a little more. I've taken the time to delete her texts without opening them.

It's not Natalie's fault. She has no idea. I've picked up my phone so many times and pulled her contact information up, intending to tell her everything, but each time, I stopped myself. She's had enough heartache the past few months. She doesn't need me tossing my problems into her lap.

And now she's in labor. I'm concerned because the baby is early. Viktor is by her side, so he'll take care of her, and I trust Dr. Young will ensure Rose arrives safely. If things were different, I'd be by her side, holding her hand through each contraction and celebrating the birth of her daughter. Instead, I'm drowning in my own pool of grief from losing both my baby and the ability to conceive again. I should be happy for Natalie, but I don't know how. Let's face it, I'm a shitty excuse for a friend.

After my tears stop falling, I drag myself into the shower to rinse off the chlorine before getting dressed and going to find Pyotr for a ride to Jelena's Hope. I pop my head into the command room, and instead of Pyotr, I see Dimitri.

"Hey, kid. What's up?" he asks, smiling.

"I'm looking for Pyotr. Have you seen him?"

"He's out training with some of the other guys."

"Thanks. I'll go find him."

"Not so fast." I stop mid-step. "Come in here and sit down."

"I really need to go." I motion toward the door.

"You're not going anywhere without Pyotr, and he's going to be tied up for a little longer," Dimitri says while he's typing. "So, have a seat, and let's catch up."

I pull my phone out to text Pyotr.

Me: Please let me know when you're done. I need a ride to the center.

The legs of the chair squeak on the tiled floor. Dimitri turns to face me as I sit down.

"What's up with you?"

"Is it so hard to believe I wanted to come home?" I snap. "I wish everyone would stop giving me a hard time."

"Woah." Dimitri holds his hands up. "What's that all about?"

"I'm sorry." I take a deep breath. "No one seems to understand that I just wanted to come home. They all seem to think there's another reason. Something I won't tell them."

"Is there another reason?"

"Not you, too." I roll my eyes and cross my arms.

"I'm not jumping on any bandwagon." Dimitri chuckles. "You have to look at it from their point of view. You fought so hard to go to New York. Over the past few years, you've made a life there. Then, out of the blue, you come back here. It's understandable that the people who care about you want to be sure there's nothing else going on."

Dimitri's always held a special place in my heart. For a few seconds, I consider telling him. I know he wouldn't betray my trust, but I also know he won't have a clue what to do. Still, it makes it hard to keep things from him. "I get it, and I'm glad I have so many people who care about me. But there isn't any big conspiracy. I got my degree, and now I want to put it to good use at the center."

He studies me carefully, and I do everything possible not to break eye contact with him. Dimitri may be a computer geek, but he's as well trained as any of Papa's men. If I'm not careful, he'll see right through me. "I don't know that I buy that completely," he says with a raised eyebrow. "But I'll let you get away with that answer for now."

My phone dings with an incoming text.

Pyotr: I'm out front with the car.

"Pyotr's ready. I have to run." I jump up from my seat and attempt to make a quick exit.

"Lana," Dimitri says, softening his voice. "When you're ready to talk, I'm here."

I don't react. Instead, I turn my back on another person I love, all in the name of protecting them.

When I get outside, Pyotr's leaning against the car, waiting for me.

"I'm sorry if I interrupted your training."

"We were finishing up when you texted," he says as I slide into the car and he closes the door.

Pyotr drives slowly down the meandering driveway that leads to the main road. "What are your plans for this afternoon?"

"I'm meeting with the legal team. They're putting together their case against Damian Nox, that trafficker they caught last month." After I returned home, Papa used some of his government contacts to get me registered with the Ministry of Justice so I could practice criminal law with the attorneys he employs at Jelena's Hope. "Unfortunately, no matter what we do, the punishment will never fit the crime."

"I keep telling Maxim to forgo the justice system and let us take things into our own hands."

"It would probably be more effective, but you know Papa. He wants to keep anything that goes through Jelena's Hope within the law's boundaries."

"That's why your father has kept his position for so long. He's a good and honorable man."

We've had that argument before. I believe every trafficker they catch should be forced to endure every ounce of torture they inflicted on their victims. Then, instead of putting them out of their misery, they should be left to die a slow, painful death.

But Papa isn't a *killing machine*. If he doesn't have to, he won't take a life. Instead, he strives to strengthen the laws and punishments for these animals. "It's a noble effort, but I still think torture and death are the better options."

"And that, little butterfly, is why Maxim is the boss and not you." Pyotr chuckles as he pulls into the parking lot at Jelena's Hope. "Text me when you're done. I have a few errands to run for your father."

"Will do. See you later."

I step inside the familiar building. Standing in the foyer, I look around at what we've created. To the professionals and survivors alike who are strolling through the halls. My mind drifts back to the heartbroken ten-year-old version of myself. To the day I dressed in my sister's clothes and marched into Papa's office.

"Is Papa busy?"

"He's on a phone call. Is there something I can help you with?" he asks.

"No. I need to talk to Papa about it."

"Misha, I—" Papa says, opening the door startling me. "Moya babochka, you look like you are ready to go to work."

"I am." I nod. "Do you have some time to talk?"

"For you, any time." Papa smiles and steps aside, allowing me to enter. "Please excuse me, Misha. I have an important meeting with Ms. Solonik. Can you make sure we're not interrupted?"

"Sure thing, boss."

Papa sits in his big, comfy chair with his hands folded. "What can I help you with today?"

I open my notebook and clear my throat. "I made a promise to Jelena that I wouldn't let her be forgotten."

"That will not happen."

"I know we won't forget her, but other people might. They'll forget how good she was." I pull my feet under my legs. "I don't want that to happen."

"I see. What do you have in mind?"

"I don't know for sure." I bite my lip while I look at the notes I made. "I know Jelena wasn't the only person who's ever been trafficked and that it happens to lots of people." I look at Papa. "Pyotr said many of the people that are taken don't have anyone who loves them or looks for them."

"That is very true."

"There has to be something we can do to help."

"You are a remarkable young lady. Do you know that moya babochka?" I shrug, not thinking I'm anything other than normal. "I have been thinking precisely the same thing."

"You have?" I ask, surprised.

"Yes. I've been busy getting some colleagues together to form a network to go after people like Rudolf Sergin and Farouk El Alami. I want to make sure no one else ever has to lose a loved one."

"I like that very much. But what about helping the people that were stolen? I want to help them."

"How so?" Papa tilts his head.

"When I was talking to Pyotr, he told me your men found other people, even kids, who'd been taken from their families."

"Yes. That is true."

"And that when they're rescued, they are usually sick or hurt." Papa nods. "Who helps them?"

"I would like to get your mama. She should be here for this conversation, don't you think?"

"Yes." I smile.

Papa texts Mama, and a few minutes later, she joins us in the office. Papa catches her up on what we've talked about so far.

"I'm on board. How can I help?" Mama asks.

"Well, you're a doctor. You can help fix whatever's hurt, right?"

"I can fix a lot, yes. But often, there are things in the mind that have been hurt. I can't fix those."

"Who can?"

"Doctors called psychiatrists and therapists."

"Can we get some of them, Papa?"

He grabs a pen and starts writing notes of his own. "Yes, I will look into hiring some mental health professionals."

"And some more doctors. I'm only one person," Mama adds. "And where are we going to do all this?"

"We are going to need a building," Papa says. "And a name."

"Yelena Nadezhda," I say.

"Jelena's Hope," Mama whispers. "I love it."

"It is perfect," Papa says. "Svetlana, you have done something truly remarkable here. It is not often that adults even consider helping trafficking victims. You have created something special that will provide care and support for so many people. It shows what a tender and caring young lady you are. I am incredibly proud of you."

"As am I."

At the time, I had no idea what I was suggesting. Losing Jelena opened my eyes to the true evil that exists, and I wanted to do something to help the people Papa saved. I never imagined it would grow into what it is today.

Jelena's Hope is a lifeline, a beacon of hope, to so many people—myself included.

Brandon

I STOP BY THE FLORIST AND THE BABY BOUTIQUE before making my way to Alex's, I mean, Natalie's house. God, saying that feels like losing him all over again. My heart's heavy with a mix of bittersweet memories and anticipation. I'm about to meet my niece for the first time. The excitement of holding a miraculous new life in my arms is tempered by the realization that this moment will forever be entwined with my memories of Alex.

During the elevator ride up to her apartment, my mind wanders back to the many times over the years that I took this same elevator ride. So many of the memories I made with Alex rush through my mind. It still doesn't feel real that he's gone. But fate dealt us a cruel blow, cutting Alex's life short and leaving Natalie to raise their child alone.

Guilt at my excitement gnaws at me, and I'm reminded that Alex should be here with us celebrating the birth of his daughter. I'm not sure how to reconcile the two opposite emotions. It's a demonstration of the harsh realities of life's unfairness. Of the dreams that are destined to remain unrealized.

I also feel a deep sense of responsibility for Natalie and little Rose. I made a promise to Alex that I'd do everything in my power to take care of them the way he would. To ensure that although his daughter will never meet her father, she'll know him through the stories she's told.

The elevator doors open, interrupting my inner turmoil, and I'm greeted by Natalie's warm smile. Her eyes reflect a mix of joy and exhaustion, evidence of the sleepless nights she's endured since Rose's arrival. "Congratulations," I say and kiss her cheek."

"I'm so glad you're here," she says, her voice tinged with both relief and happiness.

"These are for you." I hand her the bouquet of pink roses along with a small bag. "This is for the baby."

"Thank you. They're beautiful." She smiles. "Do you want me to open this now?"

"Sure."

I follow her to the kitchen, where she sets the flowers on the island and opens the bag. She pulls out a pale pink sleeper that reads, *Hi, I'm new here.* "It's adorable. Thank you."

"I didn't know we had company," Viktor says as he walks into the room carrying a tiny bundle swaddled in a blanket.

"Brandon just got here." Natalie holds up the sleeper. "Look what he got us."

Viktor glances from the sleeper to the roses and back to me. "Thank you."

"You're welcome?" Viktor's reaction to my presence and my gifts is puzzling.

Natalie delicately takes the peacefully dozing baby from Viktor's arms and steps closer to me. "Uncle Brandon, I'd like you to meet your niece, Rose." Her words carry a tender resonance.

Time stands still as a surge of love and affection like I've never experienced before envelops me as I fixate on the precious baby cradled in Natalie's embrace. The soft contours of the infant's features, the innocence conveyed by closed eyes, and the gentle rise and fall of her chest all combine to form a portrait of purity and innocence.

"She's beautiful," my hushed voice escapes in an awe-filled

whisper, reflecting my profound amazement for this new life before me.

"She has Alex's blue eyes," Natalie says softly, tears glistening. "Looking into them reminds me that he should be here."

"We have a little piece of him." My hands tremble slightly as I reach out to stroke Rose's delicate cheek.

"There are a few things I have to get done," Viktor says, clearing his throat. "I'll be in the office if you need me."

Natalie watches as he walks down the hall, disappearing into Alex's office. Turning back to me, she asks, "Would you like to hold her?"

"I'd love to."

"Why don't we go sit down."

She leads us into the living room that's decorated for the upcoming holiday.

"The tree is beautiful," I say as I sit on the sofa. "I wasn't sure—"

"I wanted to forget all about Christmas. The tree and decorations were Viktor's idea." She shrugs. "He insisted that we decorate because it's Rose's first Christmas."

"He's right," I say, and Natalie carefully passes the baby to me. "What's up, little one? I'm your Uncle Brandon." I gaze at the precious little girl in my arms. Her features are the perfect mix of Alex and Natalie. "I want you to know I'm here for you and that I'll do everything I can to be the best uncle to Rose."

Natalie's eyes lock with mine, and a flicker of gratitude dances across her face. "Thank you, Brand. Rose and I are lucky to have you." She rests her head on my shoulder, and I slip my arm around her. We sit quietly, lost in our thoughts until Rose's eyelids flutter. Her tiny mouth opens, and a loud wail comes out. "I think someone's hungry."

"She needs a diaper change first."

"I can do it. If that's okay." I lift the baby against my chest and rub her back softly. Her crying stops.

"Have you ever changed a diaper before?"

"No. But how hard can it be?"

"How about I go with you? Just in case." She smiles.

We walk down the hall past the baby's nursery. For a second, I'm confused, but then I think about it. Rose is a newborn. She must be in her bassinet in Natalie's room. I turn to step into the primary bedroom but freeze when Natalie says, "No. Not in there." Her eyes are wide with fear.

"I'm sorry, I thought."

"We sleep in here." She motions into the guest room. "I can't go into the other room. Not without Alex."

After my mom passed away, Dad couldn't step foot into the bedroom they'd shared for over forty years. He always said there were too many memories he wasn't ready to face in their room.

"It's okay, Nat. I understand."

I follow her into the guest room, where she's hurrying to pick up a pair of men's boxers from the floor.

"Viktor must've dropped these when he was carrying out the laundry," she says as she puts them in the hamper. "It's a wonder anything is getting done. We're running on fumes right now." She motions to the bed. "We haven't brought the changing table in yet. You can put her on the bed to change her." I lay the baby down while Natalie grabs a diaper and wipes.

Natalie looks nervous. I'm not sure what's going on between her and Viktor or if I should even ask.

"I know what you're thinking. Why are Viktor's clothes in the room I'm sleeping in?"

"It's really none of my business."

"He's been staying up here to help me with the baby overnight. I don't think I could do this without his help."

"I can always come over, too," I offer.

"Thank you for offering, but I think we're doing okay." The baby starts crying again. "Miss Rose is getting impatient."

Natalie walks me through changing her diaper, a task that's a little more difficult than I imagined. She's using cloth diapers that have more snaps in one place than I've ever seen. But, with a bit of patience, I successfully complete my mission. Then, Natalie lifts her from the bed.

"I'll give you some privacy to feed her."

"Thank you."

I leave the girls alone and go to the office to speak with Viktor. The door's open, so I walk in unannounced and find Viktor behind Alex's desk. He's concentrating on whatever's on the laptop in front of him.

"Have you made any progress?"

"No." He doesn't take his eyes off the screen. "Dimitri's working day and night, but there's no leads." Viktor stops and looks up. "We won't stop until every bastard involved is caught."

"I have no doubt about that."

"Where's Natalie?"

"She's in your bedroom feeding the baby." I raise an eyebrow.

"For something so small, she eats an awful lot." He chuckles but doesn't fall for my bait. "But God, she's perfect."

He can't hide the awe in his voice when he talks about the baby.

"Is there anything I can do to help?"

"It's been a huge adjustment, but we're slowly finding our routine." He stands and walks around the desk. "It's been hard without Alex. He should be here," Viktor says quietly.

I can't speak over the lump in my throat, so I settle for a nod.

We leave the office and walk by the guest room. "She's exhausted," Viktor whispers and motions into the room.

Natalie's sound asleep, her arms draped over the baby sleeping on her chest. Viktor quietly walks into the room. I watch as he leans down and whispers something I can't hear. Natalie's eyes open for the briefest of seconds. Viktor places a tender kiss on her forehead before lifting the baby. It's a loving interaction. One that leaves me with even more unanswered questions.

Viktor leaves the room with Rose held protectively against his chest. "Do you want to stay for dinner?"

"No thanks. I have to go into the office for a bit and catch up on a few things."

"You sure?"

We walk toward the elevator, an odd tension between us. Viktor watches me as though he's expecting me to ask about what I just witnessed, but I say nothing. I'm unsure if my questions would be overstepping the boundaries of our friendship.

It's no secret Viktor's cared about Natalie for a long time. While Alex was alive, he would've never acted on his feelings. He has far too much integrity for that. But now, everything's changed. Alex is dead, and Natalie's alone. There's no reason for them not to find happiness with one another. But that's not a conversation for today. Instead, I say, "Tell Natalie I'll call her tomorrow.

Brandon

My concerns about Natalie have been growing over the past few weeks. She's steadily closing herself off from everyone who cares about her. Viktor and I are the only people she lets anywhere near her. When I spoke to Viktor, he said he tried reaching out to Svetlana. He left several voicemails begging her to call Natalie, explaining that she needed her best friend. Unfortunately, it did no good. She refuses to take his calls, and his texts sit unread.

Lana's shut me out completely as well. Pyotr checks in every few days, but he won't give up Lana's secrets despite my repeated requests. His loyalty to Lana is a quality I both admire and despise. If I knew what went wrong, I could fix it or at least try. Being kept in the dark isn't helping anyone, but I refuse to give up.

Love doesn't come without its challenges. Sometimes, it's messy and complicated as it leads us through intricate webs of emotions and labyrinths of complexities. At times, the path seems dark and endless, causing many to give up. However, for those who choose the virtue of patience and are willing to embrace the journey wholeheartedly, the rewards of love are endless.

Svetlana may have chosen to walk away, but I recognize her

chosen defense mechanism. She always tries to push her emotions deep inside, retreating from everyone and everything. It's because I know she hasn't stopped loving me, but rather, she's struggling with something that I won't allow her actions to break us. What we share is real. I'll continue loving and trusting enough for both of us, knowing that same love will guide us through the darkness back to each other.

But today, my focus is on another woman I care about, Natalie. My gut tells me she's isolating herself because something is developing between her and Viktor. I think she's afraid to tell anyone because Alex has only been gone for a few months. Knowing Natalie, she feels guilty for moving on and fears what people will think. Yes, everyone will have their opinions, and not all of those opinions will be supportive. But that's not a decision for anyone other than her and Viktor. I hope to get some time alone with her today to discuss it.

"Are you sure you're okay if I go downstairs?" Viktor asks Natalie for the tenth time.

"Brandon will keep me company while you're gone," Natalie reassures him.

Viktor looks back and forth between us, still uncertain if he should leave or not. He and Natalie decided that any work involving Maxim was to be done downstairs rather than in their apartment. They don't want Rose to be exposed to it while she's so young. The major flaw with their plan is Viktor hates leaving Natalie's side.

"I think we'll manage while you're gone," I joke, but as usual, Viktor doesn't even crack a smile.

"Call me if you need anything, and I'll come right up."

Finally, we're alone, but when I go to open my mouth, Rose wakes up. Her baby noises come through the monitor app on Natalie's phone.

"I'll get her," I say, jumping up.

"She's going to need a diaper change," Natalie calls after me laughing.

"I can handle that," I call as I head to get the little girl I'm crazy in love with. "Wassup? Wassup, my precious little Rose?" I'm rewarded with a toothless grin. Lifting Rose from her crib, her big blue eyes study me. "Uncle Brandon's going to give you a dry diaper. Then we'll go find Mama."

There were a few mishaps along the way with the cloth diapers, but I've finally reached a level of proficiency that makes diaper changes a breeze. I return to the kitchen with a happy and dry baby in my arms.

Although Natalie's breastfeeding, she pumps in between, so I ask, "Can I give her a bottle?" She turns around with a small bottle in her hand and a smile on her face. "Thank you, Mommy." I kiss her cheek and take Rose to the couch to sit and feed her. Natalie stays in the kitchen to load the dishwasher. It takes a few minutes for me to work up the courage to start the conversation. "Can I ask you a question?"

"Sure. What's up?" Natalie shuts the water off and leans against the counter.

"What's going on between you and your Russian?"

Her eyes open wide, and her words come out hurried. "He's only half Russian and nothing. Why?"

"Nothing?" I ask, trying to keep my tone soft. I don't want Natalie to get defensive and shut down. "He moved in with you, and I see how he looks at you. The man's in love with you." I hold Rose over my shoulder so I can burp her. "It's okay to move on, you know?"

"Why don't you put Rose in her swing? We need to talk."

Rose's eyes are already beginning to close as I buckle her in and turn on the gentle rocking motion I know she loves. Natalie's waiting for me at the kitchen island, where I sit beside her.

"You have to promise to keep an open mind," she says hesitantly.

"Okay."

"Alex always told me if anything happened to him, there were documents in his office that I'd need. I didn't want to go through them while my parents were still here, so I waited until the day they left. I'm so glad I did." She pauses.

"There were all the papers I expected, but then I found a handwritten note. Alex wrote it after we were rescued from Mexico. In it, he said he knew Viktor had feelings for me, and he'd already spoken to him. Alex's request was if anything ever happened to him, he wanted me to move on with Viktor."

It takes a few seconds to process what Natalie just revealed. I can't imagine how painful it was for Alex to not only write that letter to Natalie but also to speak with Viktor and give him permission to be with his wife in the event of his untimely demise. I don't know if I would have that kind of courage. "So, you and Viktor are a couple?"

"Yes. No. I don't know. I care about Viktor and know how he feels about me, but it's too soon. I'm not ready to move on yet."

I take her hand in mine, and her eyes fill with tears. "You have my support with whatever you choose." I can see how difficult this conversation is for her, so I attempt to change the subject, hoping to lighten the mood. "Everyone at Fire and Ice has been asking about you. Any chance I can get you to visit? Maybe bring your half-Russian with you?"

"Bring me where?" Viktor asks, coming up behind us.

"I didn't hear you come in." Natalie looks up at him and smiles.

"I was just asking Natalie if there's any chance she'd come down to the club. Of course, you can tag along, too." I smirk.

Viktor locks eyes with Natalie. "Is that something you want?"

"Thanks again for the invite," Natalie says, giving me a small smile. "But I don't think so."

"Suit yourself." Everyone's been asking about her. Going out for an evening would do her a world of good. The invitation is out there. Hopefully, she'll change her mind after she has some time to consider it. "How are things coming with Jelena's Hope-NYC?"

"Everything's a mess." Natalie sighs loudly. "We've had a hard time getting a contractor willing to fix the damage caused by the explosion. That's put everything behind with permits and licensing—I don't know all the details. Viktor's been handling it all." She motions to the man who's stepped away and is picking up the baby, who just started fussing.

"Sounds like a headache."

"It is," Viktor agrees. "Needless to say, the grand opening's been postponed indefinitely."

"I'm sorry. I know how much this project means to you." My phone's alarm goes off, and I check the time. "Shit. I'm going to be late. I have a meeting in an hour." I get up and give Natalie a peck on the cheek. "Hang in there. I'll see you soon."

"I'll walk you out." Viktor passes Rose to Natalie and follows me to the elevator. Once we're out of earshot, he says, "She told you."

"How did you know?"

"I can tell from the way you're looking at me. I'm sure you disapprove."

"That's where you're wrong." I look over his shoulder at Natalie, sitting at the island, rocking the baby. She seems so lonely. I hope to God Alex knew what he was doing when he set this arrangement up. "You love her almost as much as Alex did." Viktor raises an eyebrow. "If he trusted you with hers and the baby's life, then so do I."

"You can be a pain in the ass sometimes, but I think we'll keep you around." Viktor chuckles.

I step inside the elevator, shaking my head. "I'll see you next week."

"I'll count on that." Viktor gives me a reassuring smile as the elevator's doors close.

Svetlana

BRANDON: I'M NOT GOING AWAY. WE NEED TO TALK.

Every day for the past nine months, Brandon texts or calls, and every day, I ignore him. He wants to get back together. But as much as I want that, it can never be. Today, he's being more persistent than usual. I'm guessing he found out I'm not on the plane with my parents to celebrate the grand opening of Jelena's Hope-NYC.

Brandon: This has gone on long enough. You have to stop shutting me out.

He's right. For both our sakes, this needs to stop.

My hands tremble as I bring up Brandon's contact and tap the screen. The line rings once, and he picks up.

"Svetlana?"

"Yes."

"It's so good to hear your voice. I've missed you," he says, his voice deep and soft.

I want to tell him how badly I miss him, too. "You're right. We do need to talk."

"Why didn't you come to New York with Maxim and Irina?"

"The legal team I'm on is in the middle of a trial. I'm unable to get time off."

"It's the weekend. Even in Russia, courts aren't in session." He calls me out on my poor excuse. "Now, tell me the truth."

I take a deep breath and say, "I want to be released from the contract."

"What do you mean?"

"Before I came home, we tried to renegotiate our contract, and it didn't work." I squeeze my eyes shut and swallow over the lump in my throat. "It's time to accept that we've grown apart. We need to move on."

"You packed your things and left with no explanation. That's not growing apart," he says, raising his voice. "Lana, talk to me. Tell me what the hell went wrong so we can work through it."

"We had a good run, but we want different things." Tears pool in my eyes, but I keep fighting the urge to break down. I can't let him hear me cry. He needs to hate me so he can move on. "The sooner you accept what I already know, the better."

"So, that's it? After everything we've been through, everything I thought we meant to each other, you're done?"

"Yes." I bring a fist to my mouth, trying to hold back the sob that threatens to escape. "I'm asking you to end our contract and release me."

There's a long pause. "You're released," Brandon says softly.

"Goodbye, Brandon." I disconnect the call and double over from the force of the physical pain. A piece of my soul will forever remain with him.

Svetlana

MY WORLD IS NOTHING BUT A DARK ABYSS OF SELF-hatred and loneliness. I was the one who asked to be released, but part of me thought, hoped, that Brandon didn't mean it. That the next day he'd leave me a voicemail and a text like he has for months. Or he'd show up at our door one day to fight for us. But each day, the sun rises and sets without any calls. My texts have been silent.

It's really over.

This was what I forced to happen. I needed Brandon to leave me. To move past us. What I didn't anticipate was the bone-aching sadness I'd feel. I don't think my heart will ever heal.

The sky is dark and full of millions of twinkling stars as I walk our estate tonight. While I stroll, my phone rings. Hope sparks inside that maybe it's Brandon. I pull it from my pocket and am shocked to see who the caller is. I accept the call without thinking.

"Hello?" I answer, my voice cautious.

"Svetlana?" A woman's voice asks, her tone carrying a sense of urgency.

"Yes," I reply, my voice wary.

"It's Charlotte Clarke," she announces, her tone firm.

"Hi. Mrs. Clarke." She hasn't called since she wanted help

planning the baby shower, and I assume the worst. "Is everything okay?"

"No." I hear the unmistakable sound of crying over the line. "I messed up and fear I've lost Natalie for good."

"I doubt that." Natalie is good. She's the most kindhearted, forgiving person I know.

"Have you spoken to her recently?" she probes, her tone edged with concern.

"No. I haven't," I admit, my voice tinged with regret.

"Is she refusing to speak to you, too? It's that bodyguard. He's poisoning her mind—" she accuses, her voice rising with frustration.

"Mrs. Clarke," I interject firmly, cutting off her rant. "What are you talking about?" My tone demands clarification.

"Natalie's been refusing to answer my calls, so I ended up calling that Viktor. He agreed to bring her home so we could finally meet our granddaughter." She stops to blow her nose. The sound mimics a foghorn, and I have to hold back a chuckle. "We were sitting talking when he came waltzing into Natalie's cottage with a suitcase. He announced that he was going to put it in *their* bedroom. They proceeded to tell us that they're a couple now. Were you aware of this?" she asks.

Even though Natalie and I haven't spoken in months, I'm not at all surprised. Given Viktor and Natalie's shared history, which Charlotte can't know, it's only natural they'd be drawn to one another.

"No, I wasn't," I answer.

"I was horrified. I'm still horrified. It's been less than a year since her husband died, and she's shacking up with *him*," Charlotte says with disgust. "Natalie should be home with us. When the time is right, she can meet a nice boy from town. Someone that will be good for her and Rose."

And now we're back to this again. I roll my eyes, regretting taking her call. "With all due respect, Mrs. Clarke, I've known Viktor since I was a little girl. He's a good man. Natalie lost her husband, the father of her baby. If she's choosing to move forward with Viktor, I promise she and Rose will be well taken care of."

"I don't trust him. He's not like us."

"No, he isn't. But neither was Alex, and you learned to love him." My words come out harsh. "You asked, and Viktor brought Natalie and Rose to you. At least you got a chance to meet the baby." My voice cracks, and I'm forced to stop to compose myself. "It's more than some of us will ever get."

"Svetlana, honey. Is there something wrong?" Charlotte asks softly.

"No. It's Nothing," I reply.

"Don't give me that nothing silliness," she chides me. "I'm a mother. I know when something is wrong."

"Brandon and I broke up," I confess, my voice heavy with emotion.

"Why? You two seemed happy," she responds, her tone filled with surprise.

"We were," I acknowledge, a hint of sadness in my voice.

"And?" she presses, her tone expectant.

"Things happen," I reply tersely, my voice betraying the complexity of emotions beneath the surface.

"Yes, dear, they do," she says, her entire demeanor calm as if she's forgotten how upset she was when she first called. "That's when you should be relying on each other rather than going your separate ways."

"I wish it was that easy," I murmur softly, my words laden with longing.

"Relationships aren't always easy. Stanley and I have had our share of hard times," she confesses. "But there's no mistake that can't be overcome."

"What if it's not a mistake but something awful that's out of my control?" I'm not sure why I'm considering confiding in this woman. She called to complain and judge, but there's something in her voice that sounds understanding.

"If you're willing to share your burden with me, perhaps I can lend some experience."

"I appreciate the offer, but it's too late. There's nothing to fix," I say quietly.

"I don't believe it's ever too late. If you change your mind and want to talk, you can always call me," Charlotte offers.

I thank her and end the call.

Looking out across our property, fireflies dot the landscape, and katydids call back and forth. Charlotte's call unsettled me, and I'm not ready to go inside. I need space to think, so I take the path toward my old treehouse. It's a place I haven't visited in years.

When I get to it, I'm surprised to see the ladder still in place. I climb up the rickety rungs and pop my head through the opening in the floor. The bright moonlight streams in through the window that's framed by tiny green shutters. The walls are a patchwork of weathered wood that has acquired a warm, honeyed hue.

I crawl inside and lean against one of the walls. With my eyes closed, I reminisce about the crayon pictures Jelena and I drew of fantastical creatures and magic castles. We spent hours up here telling make-believe stories and then tacked our masterpieces to the walls. Today, only small pieces of torn, yellowed paper remain. If I concentrate hard enough, I can hear her whispered secrets of all the adventures we'd one day take together.

"Here you are, little butterfly." Pyotr's voice startles me. "Your father was worried and sent me to look for you."

He sits next to me and puts his arm out. I move closer and rest my head on his chest. Instantly, I'm enveloped in familiar feelings of safety and peace.

"Jelena and I made so many memories in this treehouse," I say, wiping a stray tear. "When I found out I was pregnant, I couldn't wait to bring my baby here. Now, I'll never have that chance."

"How much longer are you going to keep trying to do this alone?" Pyotr asks quietly. "You need to tell Brandon."

"We aren't together anymore," I declare, my voice steady but tinged with sadness.

"What do you mean?" Pyotr asks, her tone filled with confusion.

"I broke things off with Brandon and never plan on telling him," I admit, my voice firm but troubled.

"That's not right. The man has a right to know he had a child," he insists, his tone stern and unwavering.

"It's not that easy. You don't understand," I argue, frustration creeping into my voice.

"You're right. I don't." Pyotr's voice grows stern. "You asked for time, and I gave that to you, hoping that after you healed some, you'd see reason. But the more time that passes, the more distant you become. Now, you're saying you broke up and have no intention of ever telling him. Help me understand, butterfly." I push off his chest, trying to escape, but he tightens his hold. "No. You're not running. It's time to tell me what's really going on.

"Pyotr." He gives me a look that says I'm not getting out of this without confessing everything. I lower my voice and explain, "Years ago, Brandon had a submissive." I tell him the story of that terrible night at the club. "He didn't know she was pregnant until it was too late. I can't put him through that again."

"That's unfortunate, but it doesn't change anything between you and him. You don't get to unilaterally decide what information Brandon's allowed to know." Pyotr's reprimand takes me back. He must notice because he takes my hand in his. "The man loves you. Whether or not you can give him children isn't going to change his feelings for you."

"What if he stays with me out of pity and never gets to have a child of his own?" I express, my voice laden with worry.

"I don't think you're giving him enough credit," Pyotr counters, his tone firm and reassuring.

"What if knowing the truth changes how he feels about me?" I ask quietly, my voice barely audible.

"That's a bridge you can cross if you get there. But either way, Brandon needs to know," Pyotr insists, his voice steady.

"I can't," I protest, my voice breaking with emotion.

"I know you can, little butterfly," Pyotr reassures me, his tone gentle yet firm.

Papa: Where are you *moya babochka*?

It's Papa. I hold up my phone.

"Shit. I didn't call him," Pyotr mutters.

Me: I just met up with Pyotr, and we're on our way home now.

The walk back is quiet while I ponder what Pyotr said. As much as I want to believe him, I think he's wrong. If Brandon knew I had been pregnant and lost not only our child but also the ability to give him another, there's no way he'd forgive me. Not after all this time.

Svetlana

I'M SITTING ON THE TERRACE DRINKING A CUP OF coffee, a habit I picked up from living with Natalie when Misha and several of the other guards come rushing toward the house. They have their bags in hand and are so deep in conversation that they don't notice me sitting there.

"What's going on?"

"We're leaving for New York," Misha answers without stopping.

"Why? What's going on?

"I don't have time right now, Lan. We have to hurry." I trail behind them into the foyer, where they meet up with Papa. "The jet is fueled and ready to go."

"Good," Papa says, worry etched on his features.

"Dimitri's right behind us," Misha reports.

"The car is out front. He can meet us there." Papa looks my way but says nothing before he turns and walks out the front door.

"Dimitri." I grab his arm as he walks by. "What's going on?"

"When's the last time you spoke to Natalie?"

"I don't know." I shrug.

"You need to speak to her. I have to go." He hurries out the front door.

Natalie did everything to get me to keep in touch, but I blew her off at every turn. I let her down when she needed me the most. I know I have no right to text her just to satisfy my curiosity, but in my selfishness, I find myself taking my phone out to text her.

Me: What's going on that the guys all left in such a hurry?

I don't expect a return text, but my message switches to read, and the chat bubbles dance on my screen.

Natalie: Didn't your dad fill you in?

Me: He and I aren't exactly on speaking terms right now.

Natalie: Why? What's going on?

Me: He disapproves of the way I left things with Brandon. But stop changing the subject.

Natalie: Tommy's behind the explosion. They're coming to help Viktor find him.

Me: Holy shit!! Tommy? I thought he was in prison.

Natalie: Yeah, me too. It's a long story. One that I'm not even sure I understand. Now, back to you and Brandon. When are you coming back?

Me: I don't think I am. We both want very different things.

My message says *read,* but Natalie hasn't texted back. I'm just about to give up hope when my phone lights up.

Natalie: It's Viktor. It's late, and we're in bed sleeping, or at least we were until you texted. Natalie will call you tomorrow. Goodnight, Svetlana.

Viktor? What the hell is going on? My fingers fly furiously over my phone screen, texting my reply.

Me: What's Viktor doing in your bed?

Natalie: That's another long story, but not for tonight. I do need to get some sleep. Love ya.

Me: You better call me in the morning. Love you too.

Natalie is sleeping with Viktor?

Tommy killed Alex?

My head is spinning, and my heart aches to be with my friend.

While I swim laps, I replay the events of the past few months over and over. It's something I find myself doing almost every day.

I don't know why I expected Natalie to call me the following morning as though everything between us was okay. Needless to say, morning came and went with no call. It was several weeks before I heard from her again.

When she finally called, it was a tear-filled conversation as she told me how Tommy, her sleazy ex who was supposed to be in prison, somehow got parole and was behind the explosion that supposedly killed Alex.

What really happened was Tommy orchestrated the whole explosion and manipulated the building's security footage so it appeared as though Alex had died. All the while, Tommy held Alex in an old panic room in his apartment.

Instead of allowing Papa's men to handle it on their own, Natalie insisted on letting them use her as bait to draw Tommy out of hiding. Then, she put herself in further danger when, on a hunch, she insisted Viktor let her go with Tommy. That's when she found Alex.

Tommy was high and totally unhinged. He'd concocted some ludicrous plan to get Natalie back by killing Alex in front of her. And he came close to succeeding. Tommy injected Alex with a fatal dose of heroin. What he didn't count on was that Natalie had a gun. She shot and killed him.

Thankfully, Viktor had the foresight to put a tracker on her and swooped in to save the day. He administered an antidote for the drugs and saved Alex's life. That selfless act gave Natalie back her husband but left him alone. And from everything Natalie described, Viktor's devastated.

A wave of jealousy rushes through me. How does Natalie end

up with not one but two men who are in love with her? Why does she always get a happily ever after?

What the hell, Svetlana? I mentally chastise myself. What kind of person have you become that you're not ridiculously happy for your best friend?

I've spent every day since grappling with that question. In an attempt to make amends, I shoved those feelings as far down as possible. As hard as it is to see Natalie and the baby, I've kept in touch. With one condition—talking about Brandon or why I left is off-limits.

I'm just climbing out of the indoor pool, my daily exercise of choice, when Papa comes into the room. "There you are. I have been looking all over for you."

"What's up?"

"Have you heard from Viktor recently?"

"No. We aren't exactly friends."

"Have you spoken to Natalie or Alex?" he asks impatiently

"I talked to Natalie yesterday." I grab my towel and wrap it around me. "Why?"

"Did she say anything about him?"

"Why the inquisition about Viktor?"

"He has been out of touch for quite a while."

"Viktor's a big boy. He can take care of himself." I roll my eyes. I know I shouldn't do it because it aggravates him, but I can't help it.

"When will you tell us the real reason you came home?"

Oh my God, not this again. "Because Brandon and I broke up. I had my fun in the States and decided it was time to come home." I rattle off the same answer I've been giving him for over a year. Maybe one of these days, he'll give this line of questioning a rest. Either that, or I'll make a recording he can play whenever he feels compelled to ask again.

Papa doesn't respond, but he doesn't have to. The look on his face tells me he isn't pleased with my answer. I'm so over this.

"Why is it so hard to believe I wanted to come home?"

"Things were going so well with you and Brandon," Papa says, exasperated. "Then, one day, you decide to come home without explanation to him or us."

"Everyone's always taking his side," I yell. "No one cares about what I want or how I feel. Forget it. I can't do this again." I toss my towel onto the chair and storm out of the room.

I'm beginning to think that coming back home was a mistake. Maybe I should've disappeared and started a new life somewhere no one would find me. When I get to my bedroom, I slam the door and lock it.

Who am I kidding? I don't have the luxury of disappearing. Papa has eyes and ears in every corner of the globe. He wouldn't stop until he found me and dragged me back, kicking and screaming.

I need to get out of the house. The walls are starting to close in on me. Where can I go to get some space? The answer comes to me quickly. I know just the place to go to be alone and forget about my problems for a while.

Brandon

Two Years Later...

Owen and I have just finished teaching an impact play class at Fire and Ice. Everyone's gathering their things to leave when Andrea, one of the submissives who took the course, comes over to me.

"You taught a great class today, Sir." Andrea, my volunteer submissive for the class, says. "Thank you for volunteering," I reply, trying not to pay her too much attention.

"You're very welcome, Sir." She bats her big green eyes at me. "If you're ever doing a real scene—"

"I'm not looking for a submissive." I cut her off.

I've lost count of the number of submissives who've asked Star and Owen if they could scene with me. The answer is always no.

"Yes, Sir."

"The class is over. You can call me Brandon." I smile politely.

"I had fun today, Brandon." She makes a point of emphasizing my name.

"Thank you again for volunteering, Andrea." Owen steps in. "Have a good rest of your afternoon."

"You, too." With a defeated posture, she turns and walks toward the exit.

I sink onto the chair and lean my elbows onto my spread legs.

"Want to talk about it?" Owen sits next to me.

"It's Svetlana."

It doesn't matter where I am or what I'm doing. It's always Svetlana. Being at Fire and Ice is especially difficult. There are memories of her and me in every inch of this place.

"Have you heard from her?" he asks, a hopeful tone in his voice.

"Not since the day she asked to be released."

Owen has been my mentor for many years. He knows everything that's happened between Svetlana and me. After she asked to be released, he reached out to her, hoping to get her to open up, but she gave him the same line she gave everyone else.

"It's been almost two years." He states the fact I know all too well. "Maybe it's time you let her go and move on."

"No." The word comes out too harsh. "I'll never give up hope. She owns every part of me."

"What are you going to do?"

"I don't know." I scrub my hands over my head. "The only thing I can do is change. I need to be able to give Svetlana the things she wants—needs."

"Is that fair to you, though?"

"It doesn't matter."

"That's where you're wrong," Owen says. "I know what you're thinking. Relationships require compromise."

"Exactly," I agree.

"But one person can't be doing all the compromising. What was Svetlana willing to change?"

I think back to the night we started to renegotiate our contract. Svetlana was still recovering from her appendectomy. She was so pale and weak. I didn't think it was a good time to start something so serious, but Lana insisted. I gave in, figuring maybe she needed to get her mind off her recovery.

At first, everything was okay. There weren't many changes. Then we got to some of the more serious parts of the contract, our hard limits. That's when things started to go downhill, fast. She was asking for things I couldn't give her.

Between my concern for her health and my surprise at her requests, I think I was in shock. Saying yes to anything she was proposing wasn't in my vocabulary.

"I didn't even try to compromise. I said no to everything."

"Why?"

"What do you mean, why?" I don't know what Owen's trying to get at.

"Why did you say no? Were you on a power trip?"

"No." My answer is clipped, and I get defensive. "Everything she was demanding was a hard limit. Do you remember what happened with Celia? I'm not having sex in public, and I sure as fuck will not share Svetlana with anyone."

"Did she ever mention an interest in any of that before, or was it all of a sudden?" Owen asks.

"Lana was always interested in public scenes. The compromise was no sex in public. She was good with that. Not sharing was a hard limit for both of us." I stand and start pacing. "Did you know I proposed to her?"

"I did not." Owen sits back and crosses his arms, watching me. "When?"

"Before Alex and Natalie's wedding. Svetlana said yes, but after everything that happened in Mexico, Lana wanted to let them have the spotlight. So, we kept our engagement a secret. I was okay with that. While I was in Russia, Maxim gave me his blessing to marry her. I was so fucking excited to come home and make everything official." I stop moving and take a quick breath before I resume my pacing. "It was our time. Our fucking time. Except, when I got back, something was different. She'd changed. She grew cold."

"Lana's always been strong-willed, but all this is out of character for her," he says thoughtfully.

"I know." I drop back onto my chair. "That's what I've spent the past few years trying to figure out."

"What does Maxim say about her?"

"He's as perplexed as everyone else." I sigh. "Pyotr's just as concerned. He said she's spiraling out of control." I turn to face Owen. "The problem there is he knows what's going on, but he refuses to betray her confidence to tell me."

"I'm glad she has someone like him, but that doesn't help the people who are trying to help her." That's been my point all this time. "So, what are you going to do about it?"

"What can I do? She asked to be released." I throw my hands up. "I have no right to insist she breaks her silence and speaks to me."

"This is about much more than a contract." Owen pins me with his intense stare. "You were more than just a Dom and his sub."

"Yes, we were," I confirm, my tone heavy with nostalgia.

"Are you serious about wanting her back?" Owen probes, his voice laced with curiosity.

"Of course I am," I assert, my determination evident in my tone.

"Then, you'll need a solid plan and some help executing it," Owen suggests, his smile conspiratorial.

"What are you proposing?" I inquire eagerly, my interest piqued.

Over the next hour, we devise a plan that includes taking a little trip to Russia to pay Svetlana a visit.

Svetlana

The ride to Noire has been tense. Pyotr hasn't said more than two words to me since we left the house. It isn't until we're only a few blocks away that he finally speaks to me.

"Are you sure this is a good idea?"

"Why wouldn't it be?"

"I don't think you're in the best headspace right now," he says, glancing at me. "I'm worried about your decision-making ability."

"Wow. Thanks a lot." I cross my arms and stare out the window.

"Stop being like that, butterfly." He nudges my elbow. "I'm only trying to look out for you."

"I appreciate it," I say, dropping my arms. "But I'm a big girl. I can take care of myself."

Pyotr slows the car to a stop in front of Noire. "Text me when you're ready to leave."

"I will."

"Please be careful."

"See you later," I say and exit the car.

It's been so long since I stepped foot in Noire. I thought it would feel familiar, like coming home, but as I open the door and step inside, it feels foreign. The sounds and smells are all wrong. Shaking off my uncertainty, I get in line at the check-in.

"Svetlana Solonik." Artyom, a Dominant and one of Noire's owners, says. "Maxim told me you were home. How are you?"

"I'm well, thank you."

"It's nice to see you out this evening. Are you here to watch or play?"

"I'm here to play tonight."

Artyom secures a green identifying bracelet on my wrist. "Have a great evening."

Noire is a more progressive club than Fire and Ice. Sexual acts are permitted anywhere in the club, not just on the main stages or in private rooms. Tonight does not disappoint. Moans of pleasure and desire fill the space. In one corner, a woman is being taken by three men. On the opposite side of the room, a male Dominant is being pleasured by his male submissive. In another section of the room, several Dominants are sitting at a table talking. Their submissives kneel on the floor next to them. The energy in the room crackles with a mixture of desire and curiosity.

Off to the right, a bondage demonstration catches my attention. I wander to the area to join the group, watching as the Domme skillfully maneuvers the ropes around her submissive. Her movements are fluid and deliberate. The demonstration is an intricate dance of power unfolding before me. At this moment, I'm acutely aware of how deeply I miss the visceral sensation of Brandon binding me. Of knowing I'm completely at his mercy.

"Svetlana?" A male voice asks, dragging me from my thoughts.

I turn my head, and our gazes meet. A smile tugs at the corners of his perfectly sculpted lips. "Slava." It's been several years since I saw him last. My eyes take in the tailored suit accentuating his strong, well-maintained physique. His mahogany brown hair now has hints of grey woven through it, and his deep brown eyes radiate genuine warmth.

"I heard you were in town." He looks at my wrist, and I know the second he sees the green bracelet. "You're here to play tonight?"

"I am," I say, my eyes never leaving his intense gaze.

"Where's your Dominant?"

"We parted ways."

"I'm sorry to hear that." A knowing smile plays on his lips. "Would you be interested in going to The Dungeon with me?"

A shiver of excitement rushes down my spine. "I'd love to."

Slava places his hand on my lower back and escorts me away from the crowded area. My heart races with a mixture of excitement and anticipation. "Our previous limits and safe words will be in effect tonight. Is that okay with you?"

"Yes, Sir."

It's been years since we've last seen each other, but the memory of our connection still lingers between us. Together, we navigate the club, the sounds of erotic energy surrounding us enhancing my arousal as we head down the steps toward The Dungeon.

We're stopped by a member of the Noire staff at the entrance to The Dungeon. "May I have your names?" the man asks. Slava gives our information as the man types on a laptop on the desk in front of him. "Please answer the questions." He hands a tablet to Slava.

Slava takes a few minutes to go through the questions. When he's finished, he passes it to me.

The Dungeon is a new addition to Noire, so I've never gone through this process. I hit the start button for the questionnaire.

Are you coming to The Dungeon of your own free will? Yes

The Dominant/Top you are about to enter with has indicated they will be engaging in bondage, whipping, and sensory play. Do you consent to these activities? Yes

The Dominant/Top you are about to enter with has indicated your safewords will be Yellow and Red. Do you understand what your safewords are and how to use them? Yes

Each room in The Dungeon is equipped with closed-circuit

cameras. Monitoring of the cameras is done while rooms are in use. The Dungeon staff holds master keys to each room and will enter unannounced in the event of an emergency. Do you agree to be recorded while in The Dungeon? Yes

I come to the end of the questionnaire and hand the tablet back to the man.

He checks the screen. "Here's your keycard. You'll be in room three. Play safe."

My senses heighten as we cross the threshold into the dimly lit space. Slava leads me further down the hall, and I find myself feeling more vulnerable in his presence.

When we come to the black door with the small silver number three on it, we stop. Slava turns to me, his voice low and commanding. "Are you ready, Svetlana?"

With a mixture of nervousness and excitement, I meet his gaze, my voice barely a whisper. "Yes, Sir. I'm ready."

Slava swipes his keycard and opens the door, entering before me.

The air in the room carries a brisk chill reminiscent of what one might expect in an authentic dungeon setting. Stone walls amplify this sensation, fully immersing me in its atmosphere. Adorning the walls, flameless candles flicker, casting an eerie yet captivating glow. As my gaze sweeps the surroundings, I fixate upon a rugged wooden Saint Andrews cross securely affixed to the wall. Brandon. I'm here to get over him. I shake my head, willing all thoughts of him to disappear. Continuing my observation, I spot a standing cage and a pillory thoughtfully placed within the space.

I glance over my shoulder at Slava, who's leaning with his foot up against the wall and his arms crossed. He makes no move to come toward me.

Redirecting my attention to the room, I resume absorbing every detail. Positioned on the left wall is a Catherine Wheel, a legendary contraption of which I've only heard tales. Adjacent to it rests a spanking bench. An array of crops, whips, floggers, and canes is suspended on the wall above it. Each implement appears more ominous than the preceding one.

The door shuts behind me, and I jump.

"Feeling nervous, Svetlana?" Slava inquires, his warm breath caressing my neck.

"No." My voice cracks, betraying my nerves.

"Where shall we begin?" His question lingers as I take in my surroundings. "My favorite is the suspension rack."

My eyes trail up and see the medieval-looking device suspended from the ceiling.

"Whatever will please you, Sir."

"Turn around and strip. Leave your bra and panties on."

It's an unusual demand. Slava typically preferred me completely nude. Nevertheless, I'll oblige his wishes.

Stepping back, I pivot to meet his gaze. My hands move to the zipper of my skirt.

Slava

Svetlana's hands visibly tremble as she unzips her short leather skirt. It slides down her long, lean legs, landing by her feet. She steps out of it and brings her hands to the hem of her crop top, pulling it over her head. Leaning over, she picks up her skirt and looks around for a place to put her clothes. I hold my hand out, and she passes them to me.

Turning my back to her, I set her clothes on the spanking bench. We won't be using it tonight. Then, I go to a panel on the wall and hit a button. The chains holding the suspension rack make a clanging noise as the device lowers.

I watch Lana's eyes grow wide. She's afraid.

"Go to the rack and lift your arms."

Silently, she walks across the hardwood floor. For the briefest of seconds, she pauses in front of the apparatus, and I wonder if she's going to safeword before we even get started. I'm pleasantly surprised when she approaches it and places her hands in the still-open shackles.

I quickly secure her wrists before walking over to the wall and grabbing my favorite whip. Svetlana bites her lower lip as I set it on the table across from where she stands. Then I reach into my pocket and pull out a silk blindfold.

"Do you remember how much more acutely you experience everything when your sight is restricted?" I ask, keeping my voice low and seductive.

"I do, Sir."

Securing the blindfold over her eyes, I tie it behind her head. After I'm certain her entire vision is restricted, I step away and pick up my whip.

I treasure the memories of our time together. Svetlana used to love being on the receiving end of my whip. She'd hold herself regally as I'd redden her skin. Her mewls of pleasure would make my cock harden. Tonight, as I allow the leather to soar and their crack to fill the room, she startles. She's intimidated being in this dungeon-inspired room, which is exactly what I was hoping for. But tonight is not all as it seems.

Shortly after Svetlana came back home, I saw Maxim and Irina. At that time, Maxim told me she was in St. Petersburg for a few weeks to spend time with her new sibling. Several months later, we ran into one another again. When I asked how Svetlana was getting along, he expressed concern.

"Svetlana is still here. She left her Dominant," Maxim *confesses. "He had just asked for my consent to marry her. Irina and I were getting ready for a wedding. Then, she left him."*

"Did she say what happened?"

"Only that she missed home." He shakes his head. "I called Brandon, but he did not have information. He was just as confused as the rest of us."

I understand why Maxim isn't buying her excuse. The last place Svetlana ever wanted to stay was St. Petersburg. However, I doubt it's anything serious. "Give her some space. Svetlana is a strong girl. She'll find her way."

"Yes. I suppose you are correct."

I felt for him and wished there was something more I could do to ease his mind, but I hadn't heard from Lana since she left New York years ago.

Then, earlier this evening, I got a text from the last person I ever expected to hear from.

Pyotr: Svetlana's at Noire tonight.

Me: What does that have to do with me?

Pyotr: She's on a self-destructive path.

Me: Again, I don't know what any of this has to do with me.

Pyotr: You were important to her once, and she trusts you. I need you to step in.

It took me a few minutes to wrap my head around his messages. When Lana and I were together, Pyotr didn't approve, and he wasn't shy about telling me as much. What I also know is that man cares about her. If he's reaching out to me, something serious is going on.

Me: What's going on with her?

Pyotr: I can't tell you that. Only she can. I need you to get her to talk—to see reason.

Me: And how do you suggest I do that when I have no idea what's going on?

Pyotr: That's up to you. I just dropped her off. I'm trusting you to get there before she gets herself into trouble.

Lucky for him, I was already at the club and saw her walk in. I kept myself out of her view until I considered his request. Once upon a time, I meant something to her. That was a very long time ago. Would her feelings toward me be the same? If I approached her, would she go with me? Should I even get involved? None of this has anything to do with me. I came here tonight with a plan that didn't involve Svetlana Solonik. Yet, even as I silently war with myself, my legs carried me across the room, stopping behind her.

I crack the whip again. More to relieve my frustration than anything else. If it were anyone other than Svetlana, I would have told Pyotr to go to hell. Maybe I should've. But it's *moya nevinnyy malysh*. If there's something wrong, I can't turn my back on her.

After a few more measured swings, I carefully set the whip

aside and take deliberate steps toward Svetlana. Over the years, Svetlana's only grown more beautiful. Her silhouette tells a story of elegance, accentuated by the play of shadows in the room. I long to run my hands over her, reacquainting myself with her soft curves. To see if my touch elicits the same moans of pleasure it once did. It takes all of my practiced self-discipline not to give in and touch her.

As much as I'd love to scene with her, to step back into the role of her Dominant, that isn't possible. Svetlana is not mine to have. Her heart and mind are with another man. I'm here because *moya nevinnyy malysh* is in trouble.

I didn't fully believe it until I saw her reactions for myself. Something's clearly off with her, but how the hell am I supposed to even know where to start?

I circle her, taking in every inch of her body, hoping to gain some clarity. That's when I notice a scar across her lower abdomen. Running my fingers along the raised skin, I ask, "What's this from?"

"My appendix ruptured."

That's an odd placement for an appendectomy scar. "Tell me what happened."

"I got sick and went to the hospital. They told me it was my appendix, and I had surgery."

"When?"

"It was a few years ago. I'm fully healed if that's what you're worried about," she says impatiently.

"What I'm more worried about is the competency of the physician who operated since your appendix is over here." I touch the right side of her abdomen. "So, either your surgeon was incompetent or—" I stop myself. Maybe this scar has something to do with why Svetlana ran away to Russia. "Or you aren't being honest with me right now."

She sucks in a breath, her voice tight with frustration. "Why would I lie about it?"

"I don't know. You tell me. Why would you lie about the surgery?" I challenge, my tone sharp.

"We didn't come in here to talk about my surgery," she retorts, her voice tinged with irritation.

"What did we come in here for?" I ask, lowering my voice, a hint of desire creeping into my tone.

"I thought you wanted to fuck me, Sir," she responds boldly, her words laced with both defiance and invitation.

"Is that what you want? Do you want me to shove my cock inside you? Do you think that will erase your memories of him?" I ask accusingly.

Her body stiffens.

"Why are you here, Svetlana?" I ask, my tone probing.

"I was looking to play tonight," she responds casually, but I sense she's avoiding the real question.

"I don't mean at Noire. Why are you in Russia?" I press, my voice firm.

"It's my home," she replies simply, but there's a hint of evasion in her tone.

"What happened to wanting to live in New York?" I inquire, noting the change in her plans.

"I did the whole New York thing," she says flippantly, her tone dismissive. "It got old, so I came home."

Oh, *moya nevinnyy malysh*. I know you so much better than that.

Svetlana's spent most of her life hiding her thoughts and feelings. She doesn't do it with malicious intent. Svetlana wholeheartedly believes she's protecting those she cares about. What ends up happening is that she alienates the same people she should be trusting and relying on to hold her up through whatever trial she's facing. That stops tonight. Without warning, I reach for the whip and crack it loudly. Svetlana gasps.

"Let's get one thing straight," I say, leaning close to her. "I will not tolerate anything less than the whole truth. Do you understand?"

"Slava," she says my name. "I don't want to discuss a silly surgery or why I came home."

"You will address me as Sir," I assert firmly, my voice carrying an air of authority. "I will not repeat myself again. When I ask you a question, I expect nothing less than honesty in your response. Do you understand?"

"Yes, Sir. I understand," she says in a clipped tone.

When Maxim first mentioned he was concerned, I blew it off. He's nothing, if not overprotective, where Svetlana is concerned. I don't have children of my own, but I can't blame him, especially after what happened to Jelena. Now, after spending a small amount of time with her tonight, I'm not so sure her behavior is *nothing*.

The scar and her reluctance to tell me the truth about the nature of her surgery, combined with her sudden departure from the United States, point to something bigger. I stand back and study her as I consider how to move forward.

The longer I remain quiet, the more Lana's nervousness grows. She's fidgeting in her restraints and straining to listen for where I am. Lana usually exudes poise. I've never seen her like this. Rather than continue with my questioning, I stay where I am and continue to observe her body language. The silence takes on a role of its own, aiding me in unraveling the intricate nuances beneath the surface.

After several long moments, she asks, "Are you still there?" I don't respond. "Sir? Where are you?"

"I'm here." She lets out the breath she was holding. "Are you ready to talk?"

"I didn't think I was here to talk," she says coyly.

"You thought I invited you in here to pleasure me all the while you were keeping secrets from me. Did you not learn your lesson last time?" I ask, my voice low and threatening.

"Red."

Fuck. I knew she was going to try to safeword. God help me. My next move is walking a dangerous line, but it's a risk I'm willing to take. I care too much about this woman to allow her to continue down this destructive path.

"Your safeword isn't going to work tonight, *moya nevinnyy malysh*. We're not leaving this room until all of your secrets have been brought to life."

Svetlana

SOMETHING ABOUT THIS DOESN'T SIT RIGHT WITH ME. This whole scene feels dangerous. Slava would never hurt me, right? If that's true, why are all my nerve endings firing at once? Everything's telling me to run.

"Are you still there?" I listen for any sign that he's still in the room. I didn't hear the door, but with how loudly my heart is thudding, I might've missed it. "Sir? Where are you?"

"I'm here," he finally answers. "Are you ready to talk?"

"I didn't think I was here to talk." I attempt to seduce him with the tone in my voice, but the words hang in the air.

"You thought I invited you in here to pleasure me all the while you were keeping secrets from me. Did you not learn your lesson last time?"

No. No. No.

I have to get out of here.

"Red."

Once again, I feel the heat from Slava's body and know he's close. "Your safeword isn't going to work tonight, moya nevinnyy malysh. We're not leaving this room until all of your secrets have been brought to life."

"You can't do this." I tug at my restraints in a futile attempt to get away. "I said red. The scene is supposed to stop."

"There's no scene to stop. I will not lay a finger on you. The second you tell me what you're hiding, I'll release you."

"What makes you think I'm hiding something?" I challenge, my voice defensive.

"Let's start with the placement of the scar. That's not from an appendectomy. What is it from?"

Slava's tone is sharp, cutting through my defenses.

"I told you. I had surgery," I insist, but my voice wavers with uncertainty.

"What kind of surgery?" His questions come rapid-fire, leaving me no time to think.

"My appen—" I begin, but he cuts me off.

"Don't lie to me, Svetlana," Slava's voice is tense, demanding the truth.

"I can't," I admit, my voice trembling with fear.

"You can and you will," he commands, his voice firm and unwavering. The crack of his whip startles me.

"No," I plead, shaking my head. "I can't. Please, Slava. I don't want to do this anymore."

Slava cups my cheeks in his hands. "Whatever you're hiding is too heavy to carry alone. You have so many people who care for you. Why do you insist on shutting everyone out?"

I raise my chin in a show of defiance. "I can handle it myself."

"I'm sure you can, but that's not the point."

"Release me so I can go home." Slava chuckles. "Why are you laughing at me?"

"*Moya nevinnyy malysh*, when will you learn that we weren't made to go through life alone? Do you remember when we were together?" he asks, softening his voice. "You were so young, yet so brave. When I met you, I knew I'd found the other half of my soul. I saw a long and happy future together. I didn't realize until it was too late that you were keeping things from me—things I needed to know. Things that would've allowed us to continue our relationship."

"My secrets aren't important," I say quietly, my voice barely above a whisper.

"You're going through a lot of trouble to hide something that's not important," Slava remarks, his tone tinged with skepticism.

Physical exhaustion's beginning to set in, and I drop my head, my energy waning.

"As soon as you tell me, I'll release you and send you on your way," Slava offers, his voice firm yet reassuring.

"It's not that simple," I murmur, my voice trembling with uncertainty.

"What's not that simple?" Slava presses, his presence looming over me.

"I can't," I reply, my voice strained with emotion.

"You can." He's standing so close it feels suffocating. "Tell me, Svetlana," he urges, his tone intense.

"No," I refuse, my voice growing weaker.

"You don't have to do this alone," Slava assures me, his words gentle yet insistent. "I'm right here. Allow me to help you."

"You can't help me," I protest, tears slipping down my cheeks. "Nobody can help me."

"The hardest part is saying the words," Slava notes, his voice softening.

"I'm scared," I confess, my vulnerability laid bare in my trembling voice.

"I'll keep you safe," Slava croons, his voice soothing. "All you need to do is trust me."

"I was pregnant and miscarried," I admit, my words strained with the weight of sorrow. The damn holding back my emotions bursts, and I struggle through the rest of my confession. "There were complications. When I woke from the surgery, I was told I couldn't conceive another child."

Slava quickly releases my arms, and I collapse into his embrace. We sink to the floor as I continue to cry.

"I'm so sorry, *moya nevinnyy malysh*. I'm so very sorry." He kisses my forehead. "This is something you should not have to face alone. Why isn't your Dominant by your side?"

"He doesn't know."

"What do you mean he doesn't know?"

Even though I feel as though I'm betraying Brandon's trust by telling Slava about his past, I have to do it. Revealing this hidden chapter is the only way to explain my silence and why I left him. Slava rubs gentle circles on my back. I struggle with sobs that hitch my breath as I try to tell the rest of the story. "I thought after all this time it would stop hurting, but it hasn't. It hurts worse."

"Loving someone, truly loving them, is never easy," Slava says, his voice soft and comforting. "Opening your heart and allowing yourself to be vulnerable is frightening. It means you might get hurt."

"Knowing what we lost was hard enough on me. I can't do that to Brandon. He deserves to find a woman who can make him a father. Someone—"

"Stop," he admonishes me. "What gives you the right to make decisions for this man about his future?" I open my mouth to speak but Slava holds up a finger, stopping me. "As his submissive, you were out of line taking matters into your own hands and choosing what information he was allowed to have. And as a woman in love with a man, you were wrong to keep something as serious as a child's existence from him."

"I was only trying to protect him." Even as I say the words, I know my methods are not the best.

"I don't know this man, but if it were me, I would want to know we created a child. I would want to know that our child did not get the chance to be born."

"If it were just the miscarriage, that would've been bad

enough. Telling Brandon that I can never carry his child. That's too much, Slava. I can't hurt him like that."

"You have no right to make these decisions for him."

"I know," I whisper, looking down as my tears splash onto my lap.

"You must allow him as a Dominant and a man—a father, to know the truth. You must tell him about the life you created together and that tragically, that little life ended. You need to allow him to decide who he wishes to spend his forever with."

"Even if that's true. It's too late. It's been too long. I'm sure Brandon's moved on and has forgotten about me."

"*Moya nevinnyy malysh,* if this man loves you the way you love him, he's hurting as much as you are right now." He tucks some loose hair behind my ear. "You must find the courage to contact him."

"I don't know if I can."

"You, Svetlana Solonik, are one of the strongest women I've ever had the pleasure of knowing. You can do anything you set out to do. But if you need help, I will do anything you need to support you until you regain your confidence."

"Why are you being so kind to me after I hurt you?"

"Because love never goes away." His words, although uttered quietly, echo loudly. As though he can sense the questions I'm silently asking, he says, "Yes, Svetlana. I still love you. I'll always love you."

I rest my head on Slava's chest. He wraps his arms around me and kisses the top of my head. There's nothing sexual about this moment, yet it feels more intimate than any of the times we've shared.

"What do I do now?"

"You take the first step to make this right."

Svetlana

After my breakdown with Slava last night, he made me promise that I would do whatever was necessary to get in touch with Brandon and tell him the truth. After I got home, I knew what I needed to do. With the time difference, I had to wait until morning to implement my plan.

I spent the entire night awake, watching the time pass with aching slowness, all the while questioning my sanity. But I gave Slava my word, and for the first time in my life, I'm choosing to be deserving of the trust he's giving me.

I can't wait any longer. With my phone in my hand, I bring up a contact I never thought I'd use. My stomach turns as the line rings.

"Hello?" Mrs. Clarke's voice greets me warmly over the phone.

"Mrs. Clarke, it's Svetlana. I hope it isn't too early to call," I begin, my tone carrying a sense of urgency.

"Not at all, dear. I'm up with the sun," she responds, her voice gentle yet concerned. She hesitates before asking, "Is everything alright?"

"No, it isn't," I confess, my voice heavy with emotion. "Nothing's okay."

"How can I help?" she asks, genuine concern evident in her tone.

"I need to get away for a little while. Would it be okay if I came to stay with you in Northmeadow for a bit?" I request, my voice tinged with desperation.

"Of course, honey," she answers without hesitation, her tone comforting.

"May I ask another big favor?" I continue.

"Sure," she replies, her voice encouraging.

"Please don't tell anyone about this. Not even Natalie. I promise I'll explain when I'm there," I plead, my voice trembling with urgency.

"I can do that," Mrs. Clarke reassures me, her tone understanding.

After we hang up, I move on to the next part of my plan— getting to Northmeadow without raising any undue suspicion. Thankfully, my parents' attention is focused on Amelia, giving me some breathing room. They're currently in the States, visiting her wherever she happens to be on her cross-country tour.

When Amelia was younger, she was easy-going and compliant. Mama and Papa were thankful to finally have a daughter who didn't challenge them at every turn. When she told them she wanted to study music in California, I thought Papa would lose his shit, and he kind of did. He let her go on one condition, Viktor would accompany her as her bodyguard. That was nothing compared to what happened when they showed up for a surprise visit.

It was her first year of college, and the holidays were quickly approaching. Our parents were eagerly anticipating Amelia coming home for the school holiday. They were beside themselves when she informed them she wouldn't be flying home. So, they hopped on Papa's jet and decided to surprise her.

Everything exploded when they walked into her beach house and found her and Viktor kissing. Needless to say, Papa went ballistic and forbade them from seeing each other. He went so far as to threaten to kill Viktor if he went near Amelia again. I attempted to step in and rally for Amelia, but since Papa and I were barely speaking, that didn't go over very well, either.

I'm convinced Viktor has a death wish because he showed up here to tell Papa he was in love with Amelia. I don't know what he thought would happen, but I'm sure it wasn't that Papa would beat him within an inch of his life. Several of the guards were forced to step in to literally stop Papa from killing him. Dimitri got him back out of the country before Papa could go back for round two.

It was a tense few months before Alex and Natalie stepped in. In the end, it was Natalie who convinced Papa to allow them to continue to see one another. Since then, Viktor has been on the road with her and her band, Beautiful Division, as they tour the country.

Fortunately, the timing of their trip is working in my favor. Now, I have to get Pyotr on board, and I'll be in the clear.

Me: Are you busy?

Pyotr: Not at the current second. Why?

Me: Are you in the main house?

Pyotr: I'm in the command room.

Me: Are you alone?

Pyotr: Yes.

Me: I'll be down in a minute.

I hurry downstairs, hoping I can get Pyotr to go along with my plan. Skidding to a stop outside the door, I poke my head into the room, making sure he's still alone.

"It's just me," he says without turning around, his tone casual yet guarded.

"How do you do that?" I inquire as I walk in and sit next to him, my curiosity piqued.

"Your father pays me good money to be aware of everything," he explains matter-of-factly, his voice tinged with a hint of pride.

"Right." I fidget with my phone, trying to figure out what I'm going to say, my nerves getting the best of me.

"You're going to drive me crazy," Pyotr remarks, his hand shooting out to stop mine. "What's wrong?"

"Nothing," I reply automatically, but his penetrating gaze makes me reconsider.

"Mhm." He stops what he's doing and turns to face me, his expression serious. "The truth this time."

I take a deep breath, steeling myself. "I need you to bring me to Northmeadow."

"Missouri?" he clarifies, sounding surprised.

"Unless you know of another Northmeadow," I retort with a chuckle, trying to lighten the mood.

"Are you going to visit Natalie?" he asks, his voice tinged with relief.

"No. I'm going to stay with Charlotte and Stanley for a little while." Pyotr looks at me like I've gone mad. "It's a long story, and I can fill you in on the plane. I need you to go with me, but you can't tell Papa or anyone where we are."

"I have a lot of questions. Let's start with the bit about the plane. What plane might you be referring to because your father's jet is not in Russia."

"I have two first-class seats on Horizon Airlines for—" I check the time on my phone. "Eight hours from now."

"What the absolute fuck have you gone and done?" Pyotr demands, his voice filled with disbelief, shaking his head in frustration.

"Can I tell you something without you freaking out on me?" I ask cautiously, bracing myself for his reaction.

"Do I ever freak out on you?" he deadpans, his expression unreadable.

"Slava was at the club last night," I confess, my voice trembling slightly.

He sits back and crosses his arms, his demeanor tense. "Go on."

"He brought me to The Dungeon for a scene," I continue, my words rushed.

"That motherfu—" Pyotr starts, but I cut him off before he can say more.

"Nothing happened," I interject quickly, desperation evident in my tone. "We just talked."

"And?" Pyotr prompts, his expression expectant, waiting for me to continue.

"I told him about the baby. And the surgery." Pyotr doesn't react, so I continue, "I know that I need to deal with what happened and that I have to tell Brandon. That's why I'm going to Northmeadow. I need time to heal, and for some reason, I feel drawn to Charlotte to do that."

"That woman is the most judgmental person I've ever met. And you want to go to her for help?"

"I can't explain it. It's just a feeling I have in here." I place my palm over my heart. "Will you take me?"

"And cover for you?"

"Yes." I don't break eye contact with him.

"Fine." He stands and walks toward the door. "Little butterfly, if you try to run, I'll call Brandon and tell him myself."

"I won't run. You have my word."

Nearly twenty-four hours later, Pyotr's pulling the rental car into Charlotte and Stanley's driveway. He turns the engine off and moves to open the door.

"Wait," I say and grab his arm. "Before we go in, I want to apologize."

"For what?"

"Ever since I was a little girl, I used you to keep my secrets and protect me from facing anything I didn't want to deal with." I let my hand drop. "I know how wrong I was to continually put you in that position. I'm giving you my word that this trip represents the end of using you as my shield. When we leave here, it'll be to first come clean with Brandon and then with everyone else."

For so many years, I complained and acted like a spoiled brat because of Pyotr's presence in my life. He's been there for every significant moment—good and bad. We've shared laughs, fought with one another, and I've cried in his arms more times than I can count. He's seen me at my very worst, yet he's never turned his back on me. He's never betrayed my trust. Pyotr's so much more than a bodyguard Papa pays. He's one of my best friends.

"I've never been more proud of you, little butterfly." Pyotr leans over and places a gentle kiss on my forehead.

This moment, right now, him looking at me with pure pride in his eyes, is one I'll cherish forever.

Svetlana

"You didn't have to go through all this trouble for us," I say as I take another bite of the delicious tomato sandwich.

"It's no trouble," Charlotte says as she fills my glass of sweet tea.

It's clear where Natalie gets her love of hosting from.

"Where can I put these?" Pyotr asks as he comes into the kitchen carrying our bags.

"Svetlana will be in Natalie's room, first door on the left. You can stay in Michael's room. It's the last door on the right." She turns to look at me and lowers her voice. "Call me old fashioned, but I don't allow sharing a bed under our roof before marriage."

"There's nothing to worry about," I giggle. "Pyotr and I aren't a couple."

"He's always with you, so I just assumed."

"Pyotr's my bodyguard. Has been since I was a little girl."

Charlotte pulls out the worn wooden chair next to me and sits. "I don't understand why everyone has bodyguards."

I came here on a mission to tell the truth, so I'll be as honest with Charlotte as I'm able. "Papa works with a large network of people who are fighting against human trafficking." I study her reaction carefully before continuing. "When I was ten years old, my sister, Jelena, was kidnapped and sold to traffickers." She gasps and covers her mouth with her hands. "Papa did everything in his power to find her, but it was too late when he did. She'd already been killed."

"I'm so very sorry," Charlotte says. She pauses, and I can visibly see her making the connection. "Jelena. As in Jelena's Hope?"

I nod. "Yes. We started *Nadezhda Yeleny,* Jelena's Hope, as a way for our family to heal."

"By helping others." Charlotte wipes her eyes. "That's a beautiful way to honor your sister's memory. And it explains more about what Alex and Natalie are doing in New York."

"Yes, it does." I smile.

"I still don't understand the need for a bodyguard, though."

"There's a lot of money in trafficking. When these people find out Papa and his associates are after them, they're quite unhappy. Papa has had people try to come after him because of it," I explain. "So, to keep everyone he loves safe, he insists we always have security with us."

"I wish someone would've explained this to me years ago instead of keeping me in the dark."

"None of us were certain how you'd feel about Papa's job. But you're right. Instead of keeping the truth from you, we should've allowed you to form your own opinions. I'm sorry for my part in that."

"I appreciate that, sweetheart." Charlotte pats my hand.

"Can I help you clean up?"

"We can leave the dishes in the sink for now," she says and stands. "Would you care to help me gather vegetables from the garden for tonight's dinner?"

"I've never done that before, but I'd love to."

I've been in Northmeadow for about a week. This time, I'm allowing myself to relax and breathe. To embrace small-town life. And I'm finding I quite like it.

The Clarkes have retired from working at their pharmacy. Stanley drives into town once or twice a week to check on the store. I think he misses the job he used to do.

A few days a week, Charlotte disappears to some unknown location, but mostly, she busies herself at home, something I thought would be mundane, but I was wrong. Each day starts early with a cooked breakfast followed by a two-mile walk. It isn't the daily run I'm used to, but it's surprisingly invigorating just the same.

After our walk, Charlotte spends a few hours housecleaning. Although I'm not exactly sure what she's cleaning because everything's already spotless. Today, I'm hanging the bed linens on a clothesline. She assures me I've smelled nothing as wonderful as line-dried laundry. I'm finishing the last few clothespins when Charlotte, colander in hand, appears outside.

"What are we picking today?" I ask. I've quickly learned to love working in the garden with her.

"The green beans are ready. We need to harvest them and prepare them for tonight's dinner."

"Okay." I follow her into her expansive garden and start picking the green vegetables. "You should come to Russia with me and help me start a garden."

"I've never been out of the country," she says while she works.

"Even more reason to take a trip. It's beautiful there." Mindlessly, I pick a bean and take a bite.

"Natalie used to do the same thing when she was a little girl," Charlotte chuckles.

"I'm sorry. I didn't even think."

"You're fine." She smiles kindly. "I used to love gardening with the kids when they were little. Maybe I'll come and teach you so you can garden with your future little ones."

"That isn't a possibility," I reply firmly, my tone leaving no room for argument.

"Surely there are gardens in Russia," she counters, her voice filled with curiosity.

"Yes, there are. That's not the problem," I clarify, my tone indicating there's more to the issue.

"Don't you want children?" she asks, her question hanging in the air.

Her question opens the dam I've been holding back, and my tears begin to flow. "I can't— I can't have children."

"I didn't know. I'm so sorry." She sets the silver strainer on the ground and takes my hand. "Come with me. Let's go sit." She leads me to the black wrought iron chairs on their patio. She doesn't let go of my hand as we sit. "Do you want to talk about it?"

"No, but I need to." I use my free hand to swipe at my tears.

"Take your time. There's no rush."

"Where do I start?" I mumble. "About two years ago, I found out I was pregnant. I'm sure you aren't going to approve because Brandon and I weren't married, but—"

"I need to stop you right there," Charlotte interrupts. "I know I have a long history of being overly judgmental. I've made plenty of mistakes I'm not proud of, and I've paid the worst price imaginable." I know she's referring to Michael. "I'm far from perfect, but I'm learning and growing." She gives my hand a small reassuring squeeze. "How and when your child was conceived is not of any concern. Every baby is a miracle." Her eyes reflect kindness and compassion.

"I was so excited. Brandon was going to be an amazing father, and I was going to be pregnant at the same time as my best friend. Our children would've grown up together. Everything was perfect." I take a deep breath, steeling myself for the next bit.

"Brandon was in Russia working with Papa at the time. I was going to tell him about our baby when he got home. While he was away, I had an ultrasound appointment. It was supposed to be a happy thing. I was going to record the baby's heartbeat for Brandon."

Recounting the memory makes it feel like it just happened yesterday. The pain is so sharp it's difficult to breathe.

"There was no heartbeat. The doctor told me my baby died. But that wasn't the worst of it. There were complications during the D&C surgery. I hemorrhaged severely. The doctor did everything he could to control the bleeding, but he wasn't successful. In order to save my life, he performed a hysterectomy." My throat tightens as a sob threatens to escape. "I'm never going to be able to carry a child."

Charlotte wraps her arms around me while I cry. She says nothing while I purge the sorrow from deep within.

It isn't until my tears stop that she speaks. "May I tell you a story?" I nod. "Stanley and I wanted more children after Natalie. We tried for years. I conceived several times but kept having early miscarriages." I sit stunned, listening to her story. "It was heartbreaking, but it ended up being a blessing in disguise. After my last miscarriage, I suffered from abnormal bleeding. The doctor found very early uterine cancer. The best course of treatment was a full hysterectomy."

"Natalie never told me you had cancer."

"She doesn't know any of this. Other than Stanley, I've never told anyone." She wipes at the moisture pooling in the corners of her eyes. "For many years, I struggled with the fact that I could no longer bear a child. I hid what I believed was something shameful. I felt like I was less of a woman or that perhaps God was punishing me." I open my mouth, but she holds her hand up and shakes her head. "Even though I don't believe in divorce, I silently believed Stanley was better off without me. Then, he could find a woman to give him more children. I even contemplated ending my life."

My tears continue to fall, but now they're less about me and more about Charlotte and the heartache she experienced.

"One day, when the kids were at school, Stanley came home unexpectedly. He recognized I was in a dark place and felt compelled to check on me. It's nothing short of a miracle that he chose that day at that time," she says and takes a shuddered breath. "I confessed everything to him. Instead of walking away, he embraced me and told me how precious I was to him. He, too, was also hurting from the loss of the babies we'd created and the knowledge we'd never have another child. But what mattered more to him was that I was alive and healthy. And that we were together."

"It's different. You already had two children."

"Yes, we were blessed with two children. There's nothing I can say that will take away your pain at not being able to have a biological child. What I can tell you is that you don't have to suffer alone. You created that child with Brandon. She takes my hand in hers once again. "Svetlana honey, you must tell Brandon about the child you *both* lost. You need to allow him the opportunity to grieve with you."

"He's going to hate me for keeping it from him."

"He'll be hurt and possibly angry, yes. But your path forward, whether together or not, depends on this. As long as you're keeping this secret and carrying around such a heavy burden, your heart will never heal."

"I'm so scared, Charlotte. I've let everyone I love down. How can anyone ever forgive me?" I drop my head, the weight of my situation weighing heavily on me.

"You're going to have to face the reactions of everyone affected. Unfortunately, there's no way around that, but I trust forgiveness will come. Once you're free of this secret, you'll be able to feel how very treasured you are."

"Do you really believe that?"

"With all my heart." She smiles kindly.

"There you two are," Stanley says as he walks out the back door. "I thought you ran away."

"You silly man," Charlotte says. "We were just having a chat."

Stanley looks between us. "I'm sorry. I didn't mean to interrupt. I'll just go back inside," he says awkwardly and turns to walk away.

"Please stay." I look at Charlotte, and she nods in encouragement. "I'd like to tell you the truth about why I came."

"Are you sure?"

"Yes." He sits beside his wife.

Stanley listens quietly as I tell him everything that's happened. Surprisingly, this time, it's a little easier to get the words out. When I finish, he stands. I'm confident he'll leave in disgust, but he surprises me by walking over to me.

"Sweet girl, thank you for sharing your pain with me," he says and wraps me in a fatherly hug. "I'm very sorry for your loss."

I'm speechless. Charlotte and Stanley Clarke are the last places I would've imagined finding unconditional support. Yet, even as I've borne my soul to them, they've surrounded me with only love and understanding—so much more than I deserve.

Through their love, a tiny piece of my broken heart has been mended.

Brandon

After my conversation with Owen the other night, I left Fire and Ice confident and with a solid plan. The first thing I did when I got home was purchase a one-way ticket to St. Petersburg, Russia. I intended to get Svetlana back, no matter what the sacrifice.

That's the only part I didn't tell Owen about. If Svetlana wants to remain in Russia, I'll leave New York behind and relocate. I can do most of what I need for the company remotely and fly back as required. The goal that's most important to me is for Svetlana and me to be together. Everything else is secondary.

While I'm packing, I call Maxim to let him know my plans.

"Brandon. What a pleasant surprise," he answers, his tone cordial yet guarded.

"I won't keep you long. I'm getting ready to leave for the airport. I'll be flying into St. Petersburg," I explain urgently. "I'm coming to get Svetlana back."

"I am delighted to hear that. However, *moya babochka* is not in Russia," he responds, his tone serious.

"Where is she?" I demand, a hint of desperation creeping into my voice.

"I am unsure of her whereabouts," he admits, his tone tinged with concern.

"She's missing? Are you searching for her?" I inquire, panic rising within me. The thought of Svetlana being in danger sends chills down my spine.

"She is with Pyotr," he reveals, his tone somewhat reassuring.

"Where?" I press, my voice urgent.

"I do not know. Neither Pyotr nor my daughter will say. He has reassured me she is safe and well," he explains, his tone steady.

"When will she be back?" I ask, my anxiety evident in my voice. I can't believe Max is allowing this uncertainty to persist.

"I am not sure," He sighs. "If she were with anyone other than Pyotr, I would be concerned. But he will not allow harm to come to her. I am hopeful this separation is what she needs to heal whatever has been broken inside."

"Thanks for letting me know," I reply, my tone grateful but tinged with concern.

"Brandon," Max calls out.

"Yes?" I respond, turning my attention back to him.

"Do not give up hope," he advises his tone firm and reassuring.

"Thanks again, Max," I acknowledge, my voice sincere as I appreciate his words of encouragement.

I disconnect the call and sit on the bed next to my packed suitcase.

I can't believe Maxim's allowing Lana to essentially drop off the face of the earth. It speaks to his level of trust in Pyotr. But it does nothing to help me.

"Hello?" Pyotr's voice answers.

"Hey. It's me," I say, attempting to keep my tone casual despite the urgency in my chest.

"What's up?" Pyotr responds, his tone neutral.

"I want to see Lana," I admit, my voice betraying my anxiety.

"I have to take this," Pyotr says suddenly, his voice becoming muffled as he presumably covers the phone.

"Who is it?" Lana's voice can be heard in the background.

"It's business. I'll be back in a minute," Pyotr reassures her before returning to our conversation. "I don't think that's possible."

"I know she's with you," I assert, frustration creeping into my tone.

"Yes, she is," Pyotr confirms.

"Where are you?" I demand, my voice growing more urgent.

"I'm sorry, *droog*. I can't tell you that," Pyotr replies, his tone regretful.

"What the hell? I thought you wanted me to help?" I raise my voice, my patience wearing thin.

"I do. But I can't tell you where she is," Pyotr explains, his tone apologetic.

"Pyotr, we're ready to go," Lana calls out.

"I'll be right there," Pyotr responds to Lana, then returns to me. "Who's we?"

"What the fuck is going on?" I explode, my frustration boiling over.

"She's safe and doing well. That's all I can tell you. I'm sorry," Pyotr says, his voice firm yet sympathetic.

As much as I want to argue with him, it won't do me any good.

"Tell her I called and need to talk to her," I instruct, my tone resigned.

"I'll do my best," Pyotr promises before ending the call.

I feel more helpless now than I did before our phone call. All this time, Pyotr's been on my side, or so I thought. I drop my head into my hands. I'm at a total loss for what to do next.

My phone rings a few minutes later. It's face down on the bed, so I can't see who's calling. Could it be Lana?

I pick it up, and my hope falls. It's not her.

"Hello?"

"Hello *wassup wassup*? Alex laughs.

After he came back to life, he thought Rose's name for me was ridiculous. Alex did everything he could to get her to call me *Uncle* Brandon, but my sweet little niece would have none of it. Finally, he gave in and started calling me by my lovingly earned nickname.

"How's my precious niece and nephew?"

Their children are the light of my life. They've kept me from being swallowed by the darkness surrounding me without Lana.

"Rose is the best big sister ever, and Michael is the most perfect newborn," Alex gushes. "I'm having a hard time, though."

"With what?"

"I've been here for every second of Michael's life from the moment he was conceived. I missed so much time with Rose. Time I'll never get back. I feel so guilty."

Alex was gone for almost the entire first year of Rose's life, but to see them together, you'd never know. They're as close as a daddy and his little girl could be.

"You can't beat yourself up for things that were out of your control. You fought hard to get back to Rose and Natalie. You're home now, and that's the most important thing." I do my best to encourage him. "How's Natalie feeling?"

"She's tired, but she's amazing. Being a mother comes so naturally to her. Natalie's the reason I'm calling. We're flying out to Missouri tomorrow," he explains. "Charlotte's planning a surprise birthday party for her, and we want you there."

"I don't know if I'm up to a party."

"Amelia and Viktor are going to be in town. I may have overheard that Amelia invited Lana."

"Is she going to be there?" I ask with renewed hope.

"I'm not sure. She didn't give Amelia a definite answer."

It's better than nothing. "I'll book my flight."

"We can't wait to see you."

"Thanks, Alex. You have no idea how much this means to me."

"I think I know."

This might be the break I need. If there's any chance of being in the same place as Svetlana at the same time, I have to be there.

162

Svetlana

THE SAYING THAT TIME HEALS ALL WOUNDS IS SIMPLY not true. Actually, it's the furthest thing from the truth. Some days, I'm able to get up and go about my day in a typical fashion. But then, unexpected triggers like a sight or sound instantaneously unearth all the emotions I've fought so hard to suppress, bringing me to my knees. The pain is visceral. It engulfs me in its grasp, threatening to suffocate me.

Charlotte has been the biggest source of support. Somehow, she knows exactly what I need, whether it be quiet support or a heart-to-heart conversation. She seems to know when I need space and when I need the company of others. On days when I'm content to stay in bed and feel sorry for myself, she marches into the bedroom and throws open the drapes. She ignores me when I grumble about the sun being too bright and that I want to sleep. Charlotte doesn't take no for an answer.

Today's an example of one of those times. It's the anniversary of the day I found out I was pregnant. My plan is to hide in my room, well, Natalie's room, and wait for the day to be over. But right on time, footsteps sound in the hall.

"Svetlana," Charlotte calls from outside the closed door. "Are you up?" I don't answer, hoping she'll think I'm sleeping and leave me alone. "I'm coming in," she says a second before the door opens.

I roll over, ignoring her.

"I know you're awake," she says as she opens the curtains. "Stanley and I had breakfast with Pyotr. Your plate is in the oven keeping warm." She walks around the bed to the side I'm facing and stands with her hands on her hips. "Haven't you learned that rolling over and ignoring me doesn't work?"

I groan. "Can I just have today?" She knows what today is.

"Give me a good reason why," she says gently.

"Today's the anniversary of the day I found out I was pregnant. I want to lie here and pretend it doesn't exist."

Charlotte sits on the edge of the bed. "Today's going to be a hard day. It's inevitable that you'll relive the happiness you felt at being pregnant. Then, the immense sadness of learning your baby no longer had a heartbeat will creep in and attempt to overshadow your joy."

"That's already happened."

"Hiding and wishing away the day won't stop the memories. It will ensure whatever you feel is experienced alone. And alone is the worst place to be."

"Alone is how I prefer to do this," I assert, my voice firm and resolute.

"Prefer or are used to?" she challenges, her tone curious as she cocks her head to the side.

"Either. Both," I admit, my voice tinged with frustration. "Does it really matter?"

"How has your way worked for you in the past?" she presses, her tone gentle yet probing.

"Not great," I confess with a shrug, my tone resigned.

"If your way isn't great, is there any harm in trying it my way?" she suggests, her tone hopeful.

I said I was healing, not that I was all the way there. Whatever *all the way* means. But do I want to abandon my plan of avoiding everyone and everything today? What if Charlotte's wrong? What if I crawl out of bed and do things her way, and it makes every-thing worse?

"But what if it makes it easier—better?" she proposes, her voice soft but insistent, her gaze searching mine for a response.

I'm frozen from my indecision. This day will happen once a year for the rest of my life; truthfully, I don't know how I'm supposed to feel. Last year, I treated it as a day of mourning. If I'm honest, until recently, I've treated every day that way. As if my life ended the day I was told my baby was no longer growing inside me.

"What will it say about me if I don't grieve today?" I ask, my voice trembling with uncertainty.

"It will say that you're a strong young woman who's choosing to live," Charlotte responds, her tone gentle yet firm, as she sits on the edge of the bed. "You don't have to sentence yourself to a life of grief. It's okay to be happy again."

"I'm scared that I'll forget my baby existed," I admit, my voice barely above a whisper, my fears laid bare.

"Sweetheart," Charlotte says softly, reaching out to tuck my hair behind my ear, a comforting gesture reminiscent of Mama when I was a little girl. "You'll never forget your child."

I pause, her words sinking in as I consider them carefully.

She stands and holds her hand out to me. "What do you say?"

I bite my lower lip, grappling with my indecision. "Okay," I say finally, hesitantly putting my hand in hers.

When I get to my feet, she smiles reassuringly. "I'll have your plate on the table in ten minutes. There's a lot to do today," she says, her voice filled with gentle encouragement.

After my later-than-usual breakfast, we put on our sneakers and set out for our daily walk.

"Natalie and Alex will be coming into town this weekend," Charlotte informs me.

"I haven't told Natalie I'm here."

"I'm aware." Charlotte smiles. "It's her birthday next week, and I've planned a surprise party."

"I know. Amelia called last night and told me about it. Alex had already called her."

"You and Pyotr have become part of our family," she says without missing a beat. "I would like you both there."

What do I say? I can't just show up at Natalie's party, all friendly with her parents. I'd have to tell her I'm here and why. It won't be easy, but I realize I can't hide in Northmeadow forever.

"Do you think I can talk to her first? I want to tell her everything before I just show up at her party."

"Yes." Charlotte offers me a kind smile. "I'm sure we can arrange that. One more thing."

"Okay," I say hesitantly.

"Alex is inviting Brandon." I freeze. "If you would like, we can arrange for you and him to have some time alone to talk." My heart hammers and I'm certain it's about to burst from my chest. "You don't have to have an answer right now. Take some time to think about it."

"I will."

We walk in companionable silence for the next few blocks. My mind is distracted by thoughts of seeing Brandon and attempting to convey everything to him, causing me to be distracted. Only when Charlotte veers off from our usual path does my attention return to the present moment.

"Where are we going?" I inquire, my voice tinged with curiosity as we walk down the street.

"There's a park down this way that I want to show you," Charlotte explains, her tone calm and reassuring.

"A park? With children?" I ask, a hint of apprehension creeping into my voice.

"There might be children," Charlotte confirms, her tone casual.

My feet remain glued to the sidewalk, and reluctance is evident in my posture. "I really don't want to—"

"I need you to trust me," Charlotte implores, her voice gentle yet firm, her eyes pleading for my cooperation.

I nod and follow a step behind her. If I'm being honest, though, the thought of turning and running back to the house has crossed my mind.

We round the corner, and I spot Stanley and Pyotr up ahead. They're outside of what appears to be a beautiful park filled with trees and flowers.

"What is this?"

"As we get closer," Charlotte explains, "This is Forever in Our Hearts Park. This place has been an enduring part of Northmeadow for generations. Anyone who's experienced the loss of a loved one can plant a perennial flower or a tree here. It's a way to create a living symbol, ensuring that the memory of your loved one will go on."

"I was beginning to get worried," Stanley says when we get closer.

"I'm sorry." Charlotte kisses his cheek. "We took our time getting here."

"It's nice to see you out today, little butterfly," Pyotr smiles.

"Come on, let me show you around." Charlotte leads us into the beautiful garden.

She points out the trees planted in both her and Stanley's parents' memory and the white roses for Michael.

"Over here," Charlotte says, bringing us to a fenced-off area. "Is a special garden for parents who've lost a child to miscarriage. They're Forget-me-Nots."

Within this area must be hundreds of beautiful blue flowers. Butterflies flutter about, bouncing from one to the next. I'm struck by the number of flowers, each representing someone's child.

"There's so many," I whisper.

"We brought one for you." Pyotr picks up a small pot with a plant in it. "I'd like to help you plant it for your baby."

Tears pool in my eyes as I look between Pyotr and the flower. "Would you be okay if I chose to wait a few days until Brandon's here? I want to plant it with him."

"I think that's the perfect way to honor your child, little butterfly."

We spend some time in the garden, sharing laughter and tears while Charlotte and Stanley tell us storiesabout Michael and Natalie when they were children.

The heat of the afternoon has given way to a cool evening breeze. Pyotr and I are sitting outside relaxing after a difficult day.

The wooden frame from the screen door emits a gentle scraping sound accompanied by the faint jingle of the metal latch as Charlotte steps outside.

"I'm sorry. I didn't realize you were both out here," Charlotte says. "I can talk to you later."

"I was just heading inside." Pyotr stands.

"Pyotr," Charlotte says, catching his arm as he walks by. "I'll be the first to admit that for many years, I didn't understand your place in Lana's life, and I have no idea how a bodyguard is supposed to act." She laughs softly. "The way you care for Lana is admirable. She's blessed to have someone as genuine as you by her side, and we're equally blessed to have this opportunity to get to know you."

"Thank you, Charlotte. That means a lot to me." Pyotr looks back at me. "Good night, little butterfly." Then he disappears inside the house.

"He's a good man," Charlotte says as she sits next to me. "Do you think he'd mind if I tried to find him a nice girl from town?"

"I've known him my entire life, and to my knowledge, he's never had a girlfriend."

"Does he prefer men?" Charlotte asks quietly.

Now it's my turn to laugh. "I don't think so."

"You never know these days," she says. "And I'm trying to be more open-minded."

"Papa's men are dedicated to their work. Although he doesn't ask for or require it, many of them sacrifice their personal lives for their job."

"Your father, although loud and often overwhelming, is a good man. The loyalty of his *men—*" Charlotte tries out the word. "Speaks to his character."

"He is a good man." I smile with pride.

"That's not what I wanted to speak to you about, though." Charlotte wrings her hands in her lap the exact same way Natalie does. "Stanley and I have talked about this. It's time I told Natalie about my miscarriages and the cancer—actually, it's long past time. I know it's the right thing to do, but I'm scared," Charlotte confesses.

If anyone can empathize with her right now, it's me. "I understand that fear."

"I know you do," she says quietly. "You're probably wondering, why now?" I nod. "Over the past few weeks, I've watched you grow through your trials. Today, at the garden, spoke to my heart." Tears pool in my eyes. "I've made so many mistakes raising my children. But I've learned that I have a responsibility as Natalie's mother to share my story with her. I pray she never has to feel the heartache of losing a child or hearing the word cancer, but it's part of my history, and she deserves to know. For too long, I believed she wasn't strong enough to handle the information. That's another thing I was wrong about. My daughter is strong and capable."

Charlotte's countenance brightens. A serene light fills her

eyes, a mix of determination and hope. She takes a deep breath, gathering her strength for what lies ahead. "I want to be the one to tell her, to share my journey and let her know that no matter what life throws at us, we can find a way to overcome."

I reach out and place my hand over Charlotte's, offering a reassuring squeeze. "You're right, Charlotte. Sharing your experiences, especially the difficult ones, with Natalie is a gift, one that will strengthen your bond."

Charlotte smiles through her tears, a mixture of vulnerability and relief. "Thank you for helping me to see this truth."

"Me? I didn't do anything."

"You've done so much more than you'll ever know, sweet girl." Charlotte reaches over and hugs me. "It's a comfort to know I'm not alone in this."

"You're never alone, Charlotte. We're family now, and we'll face these moments together," I assure her.

As the night comes to a close, I reflect on my thankfulness at Charlotte's insistence that I get out of bed and spend it with people who care about me. She was right. It didn't keep the memories away, but in those moments when my emotions clawed their way to the surface, I wasn't alone. I was surrounded by people who allowed me to express my feelings. Who listened without judgment as I shared my regret for keeping Brandon in the dark and promised they'd be by my side for the next part of my healing journey.

Brandon

I BOOKED A LAST-MINUTE FLIGHT TO MISSOURI. Unfortunately, I couldn't get a direct flight and have a layover at Charlotte Douglas Airport. There's another before my next flight, so I don't have to rush. While I'm standing in line at Starbucks waiting for my latte, I power on my cell. The voicemail notification pops up, and I see a phone number I don't recognize.

"Brandon," the barista calls my name.

I grab my cup and take it to a table in the corner, where I sit and listen to the message.

"Hello, Brandon. My name is Slava Olenev. We have a certain young woman in common. I need to speak to you about an urgent matter. Please call me as soon as you get this message. I don't care what time it is."

Why is Svetlana's ex-Dominant calling me? For a brief moment, I consider deleting his message and not returning his call. However, curiosity gets the best of me. I check the time on my phone. It's eight pm here, which means it's three am in Russia. He did say to call anytime. So, I hit the green call button.

The line rings three times before he answers, "*Allo*?"

"I'm looking for Slava," I respond, unsure what exactly I'm supposed to say.

"Brandon," Slava says. "Thank you for returning my call."

"You're welcome." I swallow a drink of my coffee. "What's the urgent matter we need to discuss?"

"Svetlana. Have you heard from her recently?"

"No. She's disappeared with Pyotr. I have no idea where she is."

"That's what I was afraid of. I warned her what would happen if she ran."

"You've seen her?"

"I have," Slava explains that she showed up at Noire a few weeks ago and agreed to do a scene with him. I ball my free hand into a fist, not wanting to hear the details of their night together. "I warned her what would happen if she ran."

"What are you talking about?"

"She promised me she was going to tell you. I didn't want you to find out this way," he says, regret lacing his tone.

"Find out what exactly?" If he tells me they're back together, so help me.

"Why she broke up with you and came back to Russia."

"She told you?" I raise my voice, attracting the attention of several others in the café. I force myself to lower my volume and ask, "Why did she come to you?"

"It wasn't by choice. Pyotr contacted me with concern about his charge being at Noire. He asked me to intervene before she did something stupid. It took some creative questioning skills, but, in the end, she broke her silence."

"What the hell did you do to her?" My blood boils.

"I did not lay a finger on her. You have my word." He pauses. "I wish she didn't put either of us in this situation. I'm not sure how to tell you."

"Tell me what? Just say it."

"Several years ago, Svetlana had a miscarriage."

My heart slams to a stop, and I fight to take my next breath.

"Svetlana was pregnant," I murmur. "With my baby?"

"Yes," he says quietly. "She had surgery while you were in Russia with Maxim."

"The appendectomy?"

"That's the story she told everyone, yes. It was a D&C for the miscarriage. But there were grave complications." Bile rises in my throat. "The procedure left her unable to conceive a child," he says softly.

I'm forced to hold onto the table's edge to keep myself upright. "Why didn't she come to me?"

"Svetlana convinced herself it was for your own good," he explains. "She didn't want you to feel stuck with her."

"Stuck with her?" I run my hand over my head as I try to make sense of everything. "I deserved to know we—" I can't finish the sentence.

"I knew I shouldn't have let her go, but she promised she'd tell you. I'm so sorry you had to find out this way."

"Me too."

"Can I offer you a small piece of advice?" When I don't answer, he continues. "Don't be too hard on her. She's already put herself through hell."

"I'll keep that in mind."

After we hang up, I text Maxim. I know he's in the States and will be at Natalie's party.

Me: I need to ask your permission to do something.

Maxim: What is it you want to do?

Me: I'm coming to Missouri for the party. I know Svetlana might be there. She's no longer my submissive, and I may be overstepping, but I need to get her alone and force her to speak to me.

Maxim: You have my permission.

I keep myself together long enough to board the plane. Once I'm in my seat, I put my earbuds in and pull up my playlist. Over the next two hours, every emotion possible floods my mind.

Svetlana was pregnant with my child and hid it from me. She fucking knows how badly I want a child and how I blamed myself for what happened with Celia. She didn't want me to go through that pain again. This was different, though. Neither of us did anything wrong.

Grief washes over me, and I have to force myself not to break down on the plane.

A baby.

Svetlana and I created a child together. That child was growing inside her, and I didn't know. Our child's heart ceased to beat when I wasn't there. She's carried that grief for the past two years alone.

I don't know how to deal with my warring emotions.

Papillon, you better be prepared because you and I have a few things to discuss. This time, you aren't leaving without telling me everything.

Svetlana

I'M PACING BACK AND FORTH IN NATALIE'S CHILDHOOD bedroom. She, Alex, and the kids got into town yesterday. According to Charlotte, they were exhausted last night and stayed at the lake house. Right now, they're on their way here for a late lunch.

Charlotte encouraged me to call or text Natalie and tell her I was here. But I couldn't do it. I wish I had listened to Charlotte because I'm terrified of Natalie's reaction when she sees me at her parents' house. My time to worry is over because they've just pulled up.

I stand out of view of the window and move the curtains slightly to watch. Alex unbuckles Rose from her car seat, and she jumps out. Her curly blonde ponytails bounce as she runs into her Papa's arms. While Charlotte and Stanley dote on Rose, Natalie lifts their newest addition from his car seat. Michael's only two months old and is about to meet his grandparents for the first time. They've been beside themselves waiting.

Alex places his hand on the small of Natalie's back, a possessive and loving gesture, as they walk toward her parents. Charlotte reaches out and gently strokes the baby's cheek before hugging Natalie. Stanley, who's holding Rose, looks to be asking her about her brother because she's pointing and smiling at the baby. Stanley leans over and kisses Natalie on the cheek. Then, they disappear inside the house.

When Charlotte told me Alex and Natalie were on their way, Pyotr left for the lake. He gave me some excuse about helping Misha update the security software. I think it was just his way to ensure Natalie and I had privacy for the conversation that we are about to have.

I open the bedroom door and listen to the sounds of happiness coming from downstairs. The proud grandparents are oohing and aahing over their new grandson. Rose is talking nonstop about her brother *Mikhel* as she switches between English and a mix of Russian and Ukrainian. They're having such a wonderful family time. I hate that I'm about to walk down the steps and interrupt it.

Step by step, my feet carry me closer. I remain hidden until I hit the creak on the fourth step. Natalie's head snaps up. Her eyes open wide when she sees me.

"Svetlana?" She jumps up and rushes over to me. "What are you doing here?" She throws her arms around my neck, squeezing me so tightly that I fear she'll cut off my oxygen supply.

"I've been here for a few weeks," I say hesitantly.

"You have?" Natalie looks between her parents and me.

"*Tyotya* Lana," Rose squeals and runs over to me.

I lift her and kiss her chubby little cheeks. "*Kak moya milaya malen'kaya devochka?*"

"*Ya starshaya sestra,*" she says proudly.

"I bet you're the best big sister ever."

"I invited Svetlana to stay with us," Charlotte explains. "Why don't you two girls go outside and catch up? Alex and the kids will be fine with us."

I put Rose down and follow Natalie out the front door. We sit on the porch swing. An awkward silence hangs between us. The words I practiced swirl around all garbled in my head. None of them are willing to be said.

"How did you end up staying with my parents?" Natalie asks, confused but not the least bit judgmental.

"I don't know where to start." I turn sideways, sliding one leg up under me. "Can you do one thing for me?"

"Sure."

"Please don't stop me while I'm telling you this, or I won't be able to do it."

She scrunches her eyebrows. "Okay."

"It was shortly after the whole Mexico nightmare. I found out I was pregnant." Natalie gasps. "We were going to have our babies together. Brandon was going to be such a wonderful father. I was so excited and planned on telling Brandon about the baby when he returned from Russia." I take a deep breath. "While he was gone, I had an ultrasound appointment. I was supposed to record the heartbeat to play for Brandon when I told him I was pregnant, but there was nothing to record. The baby didn't have a heartbeat." Tears drip down Natalie's face as I tell my story. "I needed a D&C. The doctor said it was supposed to be straightforward and easy—routine. Except it wasn't. There were complications." My voice cracks. "Dr. Young couldn't stop the bleeding and had to do a hysterectomy. When I woke up, Pyotr told me I couldn't have children."

"I'm so sorry. Why didn't you tell me?" she asks, her voice filled with concern.

"I didn't tell anyone," I admit, my tone heavy with regret.

"Brandon doesn't know?" she asks quietly, her words barely above a whisper.

"No," I reply, shaking my head. "I couldn't tell him."

"That's why you left," she concludes, understanding dawning in her voice.

"Yes. I couldn't break his heart like that." My old reasoning sounds weak. "That's part of how I ended up here. Your mom contacted me back when Alex was dead, and you came here with Viktor. She was totally freaking out."

"Oh my gosh, that trip was a nightmare." Natalie chuckles. "I can laugh now, but it was anything but funny then."

"Charlotte wanted me to intervene, but, at the time, you and I weren't speaking. She picked up on something being wrong and offered to help. At first, I said no. But for some reason, I couldn't get her off my mind. Long story short. I reached out and asked if I could stay with them for a while." I pause, searching her face for a reaction but finding none. "Do you hate me for keeping this from you?"

"Hate you? No, of course not." Natalie wipes the tears from her face. "You had your reasons for making the choices you did, and I respect that. But I'm also thankful you told me so I can be here for you."

This time, it's me that embraces her, and we cry together. It's as much a release of what might have been and what will never be combined with an honest rekindling of a friendship.

"I feel awful that I brought the kids here—" Lana begins, her voice heavy with guilt.

"There's no reason to feel that way. You came to visit your parents. You had no idea I was here," Natalie reassures her, her tone comforting.

"What about Brandon? Are you going to tell him?" Lana asks, her voice tinged with concern.

"Yes. Being here with your parents has helped me heal. I feel much stronger and am ready to tell him. I'm planning to speak to him soon," Natalie confirms, her tone determined.

"Is there anything I can do to help?" Lana offers, her voice sincere.

"Just be my friend," Natalie replies, her voice filled with gratitude.

"That I can manage," Lana says with a smile.

"And introduce me to my nephew," Lana adds, her voice eager.

We return to the family room, where a beaming Charlotte is

holding her grandson. Natalie walks over to her mom and takes the baby before turning to Lana.

"Aunt Lana, meet your nephew Michael Alexander Montgomery," Natalie introduces proudly.

She passes the tiny bundle to Lana. He's wide awake and looks at her with big hazel eyes. "Look at his hair."

"I know," Alex laughs. "We try to keep it covered up, but he was too hot with his hat on, so I took it off."

"Why would you cover it up?" Lana marvels, running her hand over his curly blond hair that pokes out in all directions. "It's absolutely perfect."

I have vivid memories of staying here with Natalie during our college days. Back then, the environment was judgmental and suffocating—toxic. Today, you'd never believe this is the same house with the same people. Love and acceptance are overflowing.

Northmeadow, this home, has served as a place of safety and respite. I can never repay Charlotte and Stanley for all they've done to help me mend my broken heart.

Brandon

I arrive at the Water's Edge Bed and Breakfast and am greeted on the expansive front porch by Anthony.

"This place is stunning," I say and shake his hand, but he pulls me in for a hug instead.

"Thank you. We've put a lot of work into updating the plumbing and electrical. Things Mrs. Wilson wasn't able to do," he explains. "She ran a solid business here for many years. We wanted to honor what she put into this place while also putting our mark on it."

"From the outside, it seems you've done just that."

Although I've never been here, I have seen pictures. The original part of the building was a log cabin façade that had fallen into disrepair. Tony replaced it with gorgeous cedar plank siding. He also had a large natural stone addition attached to the main structure. The once gravel parking area has been paved and lined with Flowering Dogwood Trees.

The front porch is a stunning stone masterpiece that wraps around the side of the main building. New rockers, tables, and padded loveseats are situated under the oversized ceiling fans. Giant flowerpots, each with exquisite flowers, decorate the space. I move closer to get a better look at the flower display.

Elegant lilies add regal color, while tower-like spires of foxgloves offer bursts of enchantment with their tubular bells of pastel purples and pinks. Interspersed among them are pansies and primroses, creating a captivating contrast and a touch of whimsy. Amidst the array, cascading vines of vibrant bougainvillea drape the rim. The display is a living canvas, a masterpiece painted by the brushstrokes of nature.

"I need you to design the flowers for my place."

"We'll talk after we get through this weekend." He opens the door. "Come on inside. We'll get you settled in your room before everyone arrives."

After checking me in, Tony leads me to an elevator, and we step inside. "This was one of the first things we had installed. It was important to Leo and I to make the entire space accessible." The doors open. "This floor caters to our guests with more particular tastes," he chuckles. "Originally, there were six rooms up here. We gutted the entire floor to reinforce the supports and fully soundproof each room. I didn't have the heart to modernize the locks." He holds up a key before unlocking the door. "Each of the rooms is identical in their setup and features."

The space is elegant. Somehow, he's spectacularly blended his modern aesthetic with the historic feel of the inn. The walls are pale grey, and combined with the large windows, the room feels airy and bright. "The view is stunning," I say as my attention is drawn to the glistening lake.

"I know what you're thinking." Tony grins. "The windows are tinted from the outside, making it impossible to see in."

"That's good to know." I chuckle.

Tony gives me a tour of the room, pointing out all the room's features. There are hooks in the ceiling for suspension play, and the bed has multiple spots for restraints. A deep red leather tantra chair is situated diagonally in the far-left corner.

"Inside here," Tony says, opening the doors to a large antique wardrobe. "Are various impact tools."

I'm impressed with the quality of everything. Not that I

expected anything less from Tony and Leo. "It's stunning and will be perfect for later."

"I hope you make some headway with her." Tony clasps my shoulder.

"We're not leaving here until I do."

The party guests are beginning to gather in the yard behind the inn. I've gotten confirmation that Svetlana will be here. Everything is ready in my room for later, so I start downstairs.

"Brandon," Charlotte Clarke says when we nearly collide on my way outside. "It's wonderful to see you."

"You too," I say, confused at her overly friendly reaction. "I thought you'd be coming later with Natalie."

"Charlotte is an important part of Water's Edge," Leo says as he comes over and stands beside her.

"She is? I mean, you are?" I quickly correct myself.

"Leo's being too kind." Charlotte beams at him. "I'll be helping Tony with the baking and the front desk." A timer sounds from the kitchen. "That's the cookies. I'll see you later." She hurries back into the kitchen.

"What's that all about?"

"Mama C has been a huge help for Tony with the business and has become very dear to me." Leo smiles. The sound of Maxim's voice interrupts my next thought. "Why don't you go say hi to everyone. I have to get back to work."

When I step outside, I find a large group has already gathered. Many familiar faces are mixed in with those I don't know. Scanning them, I see the only one I care about, Svetlana. She's sitting off to the side, talking with Dimitri and Jessica.

On my way to see Maxim, I walk by the trio. Jessica stands and hugs me. "It's so nice to see you again, Brandon."

"You too. I hope this one's paying you more attention than his electronics," I joke and elbow Dimitri.

"Jessica appreciates a computer as much as I do." Dimitri smiles and snakes his arm around Jessica's waist.

"Hello, Svetlana." I force myself to stop at a greeting and not what I came to do.

"Hi," she says, not making eye contact.

Jessica and Dimitri look between us. Not wanting to make the moment any more awkward, I politely excuse myself and make my way to Maxim and Irina.

"It's good to see you, Max." We shake hands. "You as well, Irina."

"I am glad you could make it," Maxim says, glancing at his daughter.

"I wouldn't miss this opportunity for the world."

"I trust after tonight, everything will once again be right."

"I'll do my best."

Our conversation is cut short when a puppy dragging a pink leash lunges herself at Maxim. He laughs and picks up the dog, who excitedly licks his face. "Have you met Nadiya?"

"I haven't." I scratch the adorable puppy behind her ear.

"She is Viktor and Amelia's little girl." He sets the puppy down on the grass.

It still sounds odd to hear Viktor and Amelia spoken about as a couple. But as I see the two walking our way hand-in-hand, I realize just how perfect they are together. Viktor's smiling and, I dare say, happy, and Amelia's radiant.

"Congratulations on the tour and the record deal." I hug Amelia when they get close.

"Thank you," she says, looking at something over my shoulder. I turn and see Lana watching us. "Has she spoken to you at all?"

"A curt hello. But I'm not letting her leave without getting to the bottom of this."

"Let me know if there's anything I can do to help."

"I will."

"Alex and Natalie are pulling in," Leo announces.

Everyone's conversations come to an end while we wait for them to appear. As soon as they come around the building, there's a shout of "Happy Birthday."

Charlotte did a good job of keeping the party a surprise because Natalie is clearly shocked. "I don't know what to say."

Leo gives Natalie a big hug. "Your mom is responsible for all of this."

Charlotte smiles proudly.

"Thank you both. I can't believe everyone's here. How did you do this?"

"Leo and I have an announcement to make." Anthony takes his place beside his husband. "We'd like to tell everyone that we're now the proud owners of Water's Edge Bed and Breakfast." The gathered guests applaud. "We thought it very fitting for our first event to be a birthday party for Natalie. Especially since we would've never found this place without her."

"You guys bought it?" Natalie asks.

"We did," Tony says proudly. "To be fair, it was Leo and Charlotte who brought the idea up."

"We fell in love with the area when we were here for your wedding," Leo adds. "Mrs. Wilson let us know she was looking to sell the place so she could retire, and we were looking at getting out of the city and slowing down. So, we took the leap and purchased it." Leo motions to Natalie's mom. "Charlotte has been instrumental in helping us get it up and running."

"I can't believe you didn't tell me," Natalie says to her mom.

"Tony and Leo wanted to wait until today to make the big announcement."

"Let's sit and eat," Anthony suggests.

Everyone appears to be having a good time eating, talking, and laughing. But my attention remains fixed on Lana, who's at the far side of the yard. She's managed to avoid me all afternoon, but it seems her time is just about up. She excuses herself from the group she's talking with and walks toward the house, disappearing inside. I wait a few minutes, so I don't draw attention to myself before following behind her.

"She's in the hallway restroom," Tony says as he walks past me with some more pastries for the party outside.

"Thanks."

I lean against the wall, waiting for her. When she opens the door, she shrieks and attempts to close it, but I put my hand out, stopping her.

"We need to talk."

Svetlana

"This isn't the time or place."

"That's where you're very wrong, Svetlana. This is the perfect time and place." He steps toward me, caging me against the wall. "You left me without an explanation."

"I told you. We had different visions for our future." I wasn't prepared to be confronted and don't know what to say. I can't do this here.

"I don't believe that. We had the exact same vision for our future. But something happened. You shut down and wouldn't let anyone in. That stops today."

"What are you going to do? Hold me hostage?"

He smiles and laughs. "If that's what it takes." My feet leave the floor as he tosses me over his shoulder.

"Brandon, put me down." I try to wiggle out of his hold. Brandon slaps my ass, making me yelp. "You can't do this," I yell.

"Who's going to stop me?" Brandon challenges, his voice filled with defiance.

"My father will come looking for me," I counter, my tone confident.

Brandon laughs. "Maxim's well aware I'm here and has given me permission to make you talk."

I growl and punch his back.

"If you don't stop fighting, you'll find yourself over my knee," Brandon warns as he carries me into the elevator.

"I dare you," I retort, my tone daring.

"Are you sure you want to do that?" Brandon questions, his voice laced with amusement.

"Yes," I reply firmly, my resolve evident.

The elevator dings as we arrive at a room. Brandon walks in and kicks the door shut. Then, he tosses me on the bed.

"Now, my darling, we're going to talk. You're going to tell me why you walked away from us," Brandon demands, his tone commanding.

"If you'd just been patient, I was planning on talking to you," I retort, sitting up and crossing my arms.

"Patient. You're going to lecture me on being patient?" Brandon argues, his tone incredulous.

"I didn't want to do this in the middle of Natalie's party," I explain, my tone defensive.

"Well, you're here now, and you're not leaving until we talk," Brandon insists, his tone firm.

"Not here. Not like this," I protest.

"You're crazy if you think I'm letting you out of this room without getting my answers," Brandon declares, his tone determined.

"I've been staying with Charlotte and Stanley." Brandon wrinkles his forehead, confused. "I'll be at their house tonight. You have my word that I'll meet you at that address tomorrow." I stand and take a step toward the door. "I know I don't have a right to ask you to trust me, but I'm asking anyway."

Brandon studies me but finally answers, "Fine. But don't even consider trying to run."

He steps aside and lets me leave. I hurry back outside to find Pyotr.

"Where did you disappear to?" he asks.

"I'm not feeling well."

He looks over my shoulder. "What did he do?"

I turn around and see Brandon coming out of the same door I just walked through. "He didn't do anything. Can you please take me back to the house?"

"Let's go." Pyotr takes my hand and leads me away from the party.

Restless hours of tossing and turning have been my companions tonight. Anxiety about my conversation with Brandon later today has rendered sleep impossible. The impending sunrise nudges me, a silent call to venture outside. Draping myself in a robe, I knot the belt and tread softly down the steps, slipping out through the front door.

"I'm sorry, I didn't realize you were already up," I murmur to Stanley, who occupies the porch swing.

He lifts his head, his expression soft and understanding. "You couldn't sleep either?"

"No," I confess.

"Come on and have a seat," he says, gesturing to the empty space beside him. "What's eating at you?"

I sit beside him, the coolness of the morning air a soothing balm against my restlessness. "I'm meeting Brandon at the memorial garden later today. "I'm scared thinking about how it might turn out."

"He's likely to be upset, maybe even angry, for being kept in the dark," Stanley speaks with measured calmness. "But I saw the way that young man was watching you yesterday. He still loves you."

"Will he still love me after he finds out I lied to him?" The turmoil within me echoes through my words.

"That's an answer only Brandon can provide. Only Brandon can decide the road forward."

"And that's what terrifies me," I admit, my gaze fixed on the horizon where the sun tentatively breaches the dark sky, casting gentle hues of orange and yellow. "Why couldn't you sleep?"

A shadow of pain crosses Stanley's face. "I had a dream about Michael. It was so vivid. I woke expecting him to be there until the weight of reality settled in. You'd think after all these years, my mind would accept that he's gone and would stop looking for him outside of my dreams." Stanley looks at me. "He deserved to become an uncle, maybe even a father himself."

The weight of his words sinks in. "I can't imagine the agony of losing a child you've raised. My own experience of losing an unborn child was heartbreaking enough."

"The pain is indescribable. Living with the guilt of knowing I played a part in his passing only intensifies it," Stanley admits, his gaze drifting away from me. "When the police arrived that night, I knew. Something in here—" He places his closed fist by his heart. "Already felt the loss. That night, I tried to bargain with God for Michael's return. I begged him to take me instead. I'm the one who doesn't deserve to be here. My existence held no worth."

"Stanley," I gently squeeze his hand, wanting to convey comfort. "You can't think like that. We're human, and errors are woven into our existence. Which of us hasn't screwed things up at least once?" I exhale softly. "You're a good man, one deserving of being here."

His response is a pat on my hand, but his eyes reflect gratitude. "I appreciate your kind words."

"They're not just words. They're my truth. Without you and Charlotte, I don't know where I'd be right now." I take a moment to collect my thoughts. "I've come to believe that our experiences are interconnected, shaping us to help those who may cross our path in the future."

"I meant everything I said. If it wasn't for you and Charlotte, I don't know where I'd be right now." I pause. "I think we all go through things for a reason. Maybe it's to help someone in our future." I rest my head on his shoulder.

His arm envelops me in a fatherly embrace, cocooning me in understanding. "Michael was a good boy," he reminisces, his voice tinged with wistfulness. "He wanted to study medicine. Did you know that?"

"He would've gotten along with Jelena. She wanted to be a pediatrician like Mama." I smile at the thought.

"Why couldn't I see how good he was back then? Who he loved didn't change the man he was or that he was my son." Stanley's voice quivers as he confesses, raw emotions painting his words.

"I don't claim to understand why bad things happen, especially to good people. And I don't believe in God the same way you and Charlotte do, but the image of a heaven where Michael, Evan, Jelena, and my unborn child find happiness is one I cherish." I lift my head and look up at him. "It's time to forgive yourself, Stanley. If there's one thing I've learned being here with you and Charlotte, it's the value of forgiveness."

"And the student becomes the teacher," he says, his lips curving into a smile.

"You and Charlotte have left an indelible mark on my life. For that, I'm endlessly grateful." My stomach growls loudly, and I giggle. "Well, that's embarrassing."

"How about we head inside and whip up some breakfast?" Stanley suggests, warmth in his eyes. "It'll be a surprise for Charlotte."

"Thank you, Stanley." I plant a soft kiss on his cheek.

"Thank you, Lana girl."

As the sun's rays dance across the landscape, a quiet acknowledgment passes between us. In the essence of dawn, we find strength, connection, and unwavering gratitude for the bonds woven through shared trials and compassion.

Brandon

I find myself waiting at the address she provided, Forever in Our Hearts Memory Garden. The connection between this place and us escapes me. Unless it's some kind of symbolic reflection of what we used to be. A part of me wonders if letting Svetlana walk out of my room yesterday was the biggest mistake of my life.

I keep checking the time on my phone. The minutes seem to be dragging on for hours. It's eleven fifty-eight, and there's no sign of Svetlana. Impatience gnaws at me as I pace back and forth. Finally, I see her emerge from around the corner, a brown bag in her hands.

"Thank you for meeting me here," Svetlana says, her voice a mixture of gratitude and trepidation.

"Why are we here?" My question comes out with more impatience than I intended.

"Can we sit?" Her voice holds a delicate plea as she gestures toward a bench within the garden.

I follow her to the teak bench, the unease between us palpable. She places the bag on the ground and takes a seat beside me.

"Charlotte brought me here the other day," Svetlana begins,

her gaze resting on a white rose bush nearby. "They planted that rose in Michael's memory."

"It's beautiful," I acknowledge, trying to mask my frustration at her for stalling. "Why did you leave me?" The question hangs heavy, my heart yearning for her to open up on her own terms.

"I thought it was the right thing to do," she answers, her voice tinged with uncertainty.

"The right thing for whom?" I press gently, my curiosity and confusion intertwining. "We were in love, or I believed we were."

"It was because I loved you," she admits, her eyes carrying the weight of unspoken truths.

"You don't leave someone you love." My frustration emerges, and I ball my hands into fists, fighting my anger at being kept in the dark for so long.

"God, I don't know how to do this," Svetlana's head drops into her hands, her vulnerability breaking through her defenses. "I was trying to protect you."

"Protect me? From what?" The distance between us now feels like a chasm.

"From finding out I was pregnant."

Her words settle like a lead weight on my chest, an anchor of heaviness that presses down on my heart and lungs. Hearing Svetlana utter the words makes what happened undeniably real. The emotional barrier I'd erected crumbles, allowing the profound weight of the revelation to flood in. I struggle to maintain my composure while she continues to speak.

"I found out shortly after Alex and Natalie were rescued from Moreno. I was planning to tell you when you came home from Russia, but while you were gone, I miscarried and had surgery."

"You didn't have an appendectomy." My voice trembles.

"It was a D&C," Lana confesses, her voice carrying the burden of pain and guilt.

"Why didn't you tell me?" My frustration dissipates, leaving behind a hollow ache.

"I knew how hurt you were after Celia's miscarriage and how much you wanted a baby," she says as tears slide down her cheeks.

"Creating life with you wasn't enough of a reason to tell me?" I take a deep breath, wrestling to control my emotions.

"There's more," her voice softens, and I brace myself for what's to come. "The surgery didn't go as planned. There were major complications." Her breath catches on a sob. "I started hemorrhaging, and the doctor couldn't stop it. He had to do an emergency hysterectomy." Her cerulean eyes lock with mine, revealing her hidden torment. "I can't give you a child."

Her words land like a hammer blow to my heart. An ache reverberates through every fiber of my being.

Svetlana's gaze remains fixed on mine, her tears revealing the pain she's carried for so long. "I understand if you're angry and can't forgive me. I'll accept whatever punishment you deem fit."

Speechless, I stare at her, a whirlwind of emotions stirring within me. The revelation she's laid bare hangs between us. The thought that she believes her confession will be met with punishment tugs at my heartstrings. Still, I feel anger at her choices. "Leaving was easier than the truth?" My voice is a whisper.

"I believed you deserved a chance at a life with someone who could give you children."

"Did I not deserve to know about our child? To make my own choices about our future?" My voice quivers with the weight of my emotions, and I'm forced to look away.

"Yes, you did. And I took that from you," Lana admits. "It isn't enough to say I'm sorry, but that's all I have." She wipes at the tears pouring down her face.

"*Papillon*, I'm hurt that you didn't tell me. That we didn't have the chance to mourn our loss together," my voice trembles with the pain of untold sorrow. She tries to turn away from me, but I grasp her shoulders, not letting her. "It wasn't just your loss. It's our loss, Svetlana."

Svetlana has carried the burden of this heart-wrenching secret alone. The isolation she must have felt, grappling with the unimaginable loss of our child. The agony of her fertility being ripped away from her—she battled it alone. It's a pain that cuts deep, and the realization of it gnaws at my heart.

"I never wanted you to feel this kind of pain," Svetlana's voice quivers. She falls against my chest as she breaks. I wrap my arms around her, holding her to me as she cries. "It hurts so much, Brandon."

"I'm here now. Let it all out," I offer a shaky reassurance. My own tears flow, a mingling of grief and acceptance as the reality of our loss takes root.

"I thought you'd hate me for not being able to give our baby life." She whispers, her voice strained. "And for not being able to give you another child."

"How could I hate you for something that was beyond your control?" The idea that I'd be angry over a miscarriage pierces me, casting a shadow over my heart. "I do feel an overwhelming sorrow for the life that slipped away and the weight of the secret you carried alone for all these years. You denied me the chance to stand by you."

"I'm so sorry, Brandon. I wish I did things differently." She pulls back to look at me. "Pyotr wanted to call you when it happened, but I made him swear never to tell you." Svetlana must sense my anger toward him for keeping this from me because she says, "Please don't be mad at him. He's never stopped encouraging me to tell you."

"Pyotr and I will talk, but not now."

"It was actually Slava who convinced me to come forward," she continues her admission as if to reveal the layers of deception one by one.

"Go on," I prompt, my hope swelling that this signifies a change to embrace honesty over secrecy.

"I went to Noire looking to play. Hoping it would numb the pain. Slava showed up and asked me to do a scene with him. It wasn't until later that I found out that Pyotr had called him, concerned about my well-being, and asked him to intervene. Slava restrained me and wouldn't let me go until I told him what I was hiding." Her voice falters, and she wipes at the tears streaming down her cheeks. "That's when I reached out to Charlotte. I didn't come here to escape but to heal."

Lana shares how instrumental Charlotte and Stanley have been in her journey toward healing. Her words shift the lens through which I see Natalie's parents.

"A few days ago, Charlotte brought me here." She reaches into the brown bag and carefully lifts a delicate plant out. "These are forget-me-nots. They're used as a symbol of miscarriage and fertility loss."

I look beyond where we're sitting, taking in an area filled with a sea of vibrant blue flowers. "That's why you brought me here?" I ask, my voice filled with a mixture of emotions.

"Yes," Lana says, her gaze unwavering. "Pyotr suggested planting them together, but I chose to wait—to plant them with you."

Guiding Lana by the hand, we step into the garden. An array of flowers surrounds us, each one a testament to the brief existence that was never realized. The weight of this sight engulfs me, and my legs buckle beneath the emotional tide. Collapsing to my knees, an avalanche of feelings overcomes me, and I double over as my body trembles from the force of my tears.

Lana sinks next to me and wraps her arms around me. "I'm so sorry, Brandon. So very sorry." Her pain echoes in every tear that falls.

Our shared heartache is a relentless torrent, and we surrender to its waves, allowing grief to consume us. In each other's arms, we find peace that binds us together.

Eventually, our tears run dry, and we stand together. Our entwined fingers outward signify our unity as we make our way to a place that resonates with our grief. With trembling hands, we cradle a remembrance flower, a delicate testament to love that endures beyond tragic loss. One that reminds us that enduring love transcends even the darkest of losses.

"Where do we go from here?" Lana asks quietly as she rests in my embrace.

"I want us, *papillon*. That's all I've ever wanted."

Her eyes search mine, uncertainty lingering in their depths. "But how can you want me when you've always wanted to be a father, and I can't give you children?"

"That doesn't change anything." I run my knuckles gently down her cheek. "Whether we have children or not is irrelevant. You are who I want to spend my forever with."

"But—"

I silence her protest with a gentle kiss. "I. Choose. You," I say, punctuating each word with a kiss. "I choose us."

That night, I bring Svetlana back to the bed and breakfast, where I slide my engagement ring back on her finger. "This time, you will not be removing it."

"Never again," she promises as her lips meet mine and her hands drift down to the button on my pants.

I grab her wrist, stopping her. "We're doing this the right way this time. We won't be having sex until our contract is negotiated and signed."

"You're kidding, right?"

"I'm dead serious," I say, stepping back.

The first time we did this, we ignored every rule regarding negotiating. We continued our physical relationship, which did, at times, influence things we agreed or didn't agree to. We've been lucky enough to get a second chance. I'm not leaving anything to chance.

"So, where do you plan to sleep tonight?" she asks, cocking her head to the side.

"In another room." I grin and hold up my key card.

"Well," she says, stepping closer to me. "In that case, let me kiss my fiancé goodnight."

Lana doesn't kiss me soft or sweet. It's heated and desperate. One of my hands tangles in her hair as the other pulls her body against mine. I said we weren't going to sleep together. I never said it would be easy. It takes every ounce of willpower to pull away from her and end the kiss.

"It looks like you have a little problem there," Lana says, pointing to the erection straining my pants.

"Little?" I raise an eyebrow.

"Can I take care of it for you?" She bites her bottom lip.

I give her a quick peck on the cheek. "Goodnight, *papillon*."

Her beautiful laugh follows me as I walk down the hall to the staircase. I insisted on having a room on a separate floor to help eliminate any temptation.

After I'm in my room, I strip my clothes and step under the hot spray of the shower. I wrap my hand around my cock as it grows hard. I close my eyes and picture Lana and how she looks at me when she's on her knees before me. I imagine her tongue licking up my swollen length. My finger slides over my head, stimulating the sensitive skin.

The hot water from the shower surrounds me. My body's on fire. I can feel my orgasm building and moan out loud. Putting a hand against the wall for support, I thrust into my hand faster and harder. My knees begin to shake, and I feel my balls tighten.

"Fuck." My orgasm hits me hard and fast. Rippling waves pulse through my body, and my breath comes in short gasps, and I shoot streams of cum onto my stomach. I rest my forehead against the cool tile, trying to catch my breath.

After my shower, I dry my body and put on a clean pair of boxers. I lay down on the bed and try to calm myself. Despite my release, my body wants more. It craves the woman upstairs.

Svetlana

The next day, Brandon and I ask my parents, Amelia, and Viktor, to meet us at the gazebo. It's time to tell my family, who's already there waiting for us.

"They're probably expecting us to announce our engagement," I say. "Why did I think this was a good idea?"

"Because they deserve to know," Brandon responds. "Your family is strong. They'll be able to handle it. I'm more concerned with how you are."

"I think I'm numb right now." I slide my hand into his and interlace our fingers.

"Lean on me, *papillon*. Let me be your strength." He rubs my hand with his thumb. "You're not alone anymore."

"Thank you for meeting us," I say as we sit down.

"Why do you look so grim?" Papa asks. "I was certain this was a happy occasion."

I look to Brandon and will my tears not to fall.

"We have something rather difficult to tell you all," Brandon says. "Two years ago, Svetlana and I lost our unborn child."

"Is that why you came home so suddenly?" Mama asks.

"It was more than that." I swallow over the lump in my throat. "I lied when I told everyone I had an appendectomy. I had a D&C. It was supposed to be routine, but things went horribly wrong." I make the mistake of looking at Papa and spotting silent tears streaming down his face. I can't hold my emotions back any longer and break down.

Brandon wraps his arm around me. "The doctor performed a hysterectomy to save her life."

"I'm so sorry. I'll never be able to give you a grandchild."

"*Moya babochka*, I would not trade your life..." He's overcome with emotion.

I walk over to where Papa sits. He opens his arms, and I crawl onto his lap like I did when I was a little girl.

"I do not need a grandchild." Papa holds me tight. "You are so very precious to me, Svetlana. I do not know what I would do if anything ever happened to you."

Mama tucks my tear-soaked hair behind my ear. "I'm so sorry, my sweet daughter. I only wish you'd told us sooner. Allowed us to support you when you were hurting."

"I thought I was protecting everyone." I cling to Papa.

In this moment of shared vulnerability, the bonds of family, forged in fire, anchor us against the turbulent winds of life. Through the years of joys and tribulations, our connection has only grown stronger. Each obstacle and challenge has merely added another layer of resilience to the unbreakable chain that links us. Our love for each other isn't simply a force that shelters us from the storm. It's a beacon that guides us through the darkest nights.

On my way back to Brandon's side, I stop to hug Amelia. "Is that an engagement ring?" she asks, grabbing my left hand.

"That's the other thing we wanted to tell you all," Brandon says, snaking his arm around my waist. "I've asked Svetlana to marry me, and she said yes."

There are more tears, but this time, they are tears of joy.

I allowed myself to believe my own lie that I had to protect my family—that I had to suffer alone. This moment is a testament to the enduring power of family, a reminder that no matter how rough the seas are, we sail through them together.

Brandon and I left Northmeadow together and flew back to New York. But we didn't go back to his house in Brooklyn, at least not right away. Instead, Brandon took me to his new penthouse in the Upper West Side, not too far from where Alex and Natalie live. It's a stunning three-bedroom home in the iconic Eldorado building. The inside is sleek and modern, but my favorite part is the large terrace overlooking the lake in Central Park. It'll be the perfect spot for my small vegetable garden next summer.

I was shocked that he no longer lived in his family home. He explained that he moved out about a year after we broke up. He toyed with the idea of selling it, but after rekindling his relationship with his sister, he opted for a short-term rental. Kendric, his brother-in-law, will be retiring from the Army next year, and they'll be moving back to Brooklyn. The house is undergoing extensive renovations, so when his family returns, they'll have a home waiting for them.

We've spent the past few weeks renegotiating our contract. Brandon and I are on the same page about everything except for sex in public, specifically at the club. He nearly went feral when I brought it up, but he heard me out about my comfort level with being naked and my desire to have sex in front of a crowd.

When it was Brandon's turn to state his case, he spoke about how much what happened at Chains still haunts him. I don't know if he'll ever fully get past it. Although I don't see the harm, I understand the trauma he endured that night and decided to withdraw my request. It's not an activity I feel comfortable pushing for.

That was the remaining area of contention, so with that out

of the way, we're ready to sign our new contract, making our dynamic official.

To celebrate, we're going to Fire and Ice tonight. It's the first time we'll be there since we got back together. I'm a little disappointed that it's mid-week and there won't be a huge crowd. But there's plenty of time for reunions with friends.

Brandon: I'm stuck with a client at the office. Have Pyotr drop you off. I'll meet you there.

That's a text I've gotten used to. Brandon is not only the acting CEO of Montgomery Advertising but also has taken over Alex's position in Papa's network. The added responsibilities mean he often works long hours during the week. I have drawn the line at going into the office on a weekend unless it's an emergency with the trafficking operations.

His demanding schedule means I have plenty of time to study for the bar. Once I pass, I'll officially be joining the legal counsel at Jelena's Hope NYC. Until then, I volunteer several days a week in the children's unit.

It's difficult to see the damage done to innocent lives. Every day, I witness firsthand the profound damage inflicted upon innocent souls. The scars etched across their spirits are a painful testament to their unimaginable ordeals. The haunted look in their young eyes serves as a stark reminder of the urgent need for change. Every interaction reinforces the importance of our collective efforts to dismantle the networks of exploitation.

My role in restoring their stolen childhoods is minimal, but I'm grateful to be a small part of their healing journey. Every moment spent in their company, each effort to provide a glimmer of normalcy, is a step toward helping them reclaim their shattered innocence. The bond that forms between us, a blend of trust and shared understanding, fuels my determination to advocate fiercely on their behalf.

The path to healing is long and often full of setbacks. But the strength and determination these children show as they scratch and claw their way back to mental, physical, and emotional health is nothing short of awe-inspiring. Witnessing even the faintest spark of hope ignite within their eyes reinforces the unwavering truth that light and love will always triumph in the face of darkness.

Me: Yes, Sir.

I finish my makeup and slide my feet into my favorite black heels.

"You look beautiful, butterfly," Pyotr says when I step into the kitchen. "More than beautiful, you look at peace."

"I am. I should've listened to you from the beginning."

"Say that again?" he jokes, putting his hand up to his ear.

"Once is all you get," I chuckle.

My relationships with everyone in my life have all been more effortless since embracing the truth. However, the most important relationship, the one I share with myself, has undergone the biggest transformation. No longer burdened by the weight of secrets, I've gained confidence in my authentic self. I can now look in the mirror and recognize my reflection. This inner harmony is a treasure that has paved the way for stronger connections with others and a brighter path forward.

Brandon

"You have the keys and remember how to work the alarm?" Owen asks.

"I do."

"What time are you expecting Lana?"

I check the clock on my phone. "She should be here any minute."

"Then, I'm going to make myself scarce. Enjoy your evening."

"I plan to."

Svetlana's expecting to come to the club to sign the contract and be collared. Both of those things are going to happen, just not like she's thinking.

While we were renegotiating, Svetlana asked for something I couldn't give her—sex at the club. Our very first scene together, having her naked in front of everyone, was a stretch. There's no way in hell I'm fucking her in front of anyone. Even the thought of having sex in a private room while others are outside was enough to send terror coursing through my veins. In the end, she agreed that it wasn't necessary to move forward.

I knew I wanted to sign our contract and collar her at Fire and Ice. When I was making arrangements with Owen, I came up with an idea. One that's going to play out tonight.

I double-check my surroundings, making sure everything is perfect. In the center of the room is a small table with two chairs. Our contract and a silver pen are on it. In the center is the jewelry box containing Lana's collar. Once we sign, I'll lock the chains around her neck, and then the real fun begins.

The front door chimes, alerting me that Lana's arrived.

"Good evening," I say as she walks into the club's main room.

"Where is everyone?" she asks, looking around.

"It's just you and me tonight, *papillon*." I pull out a chair.

Her heels click as she walks to the table and gracefully sits. I take the seat across from her. "The first order of business tonight is reviewing the contract to ensure everything is as agreed."

She nods and lifts the papers. Svetlana never looks up. Her attention focused on reading each page. When she comes to the end, she sets them in front of her on the table. "May I have the pen, Sir?"

I hand her the fountain pen I purchased specifically for this occasion. Lana smiles appreciatively and signs her name. She slides the papers across the table, and I take the pen from her outstretched hand and sign my name above hers.

With the contract signed, I pick up the jewelry box and step away from the table.

"Come here." Lana walks over and stands before me. "Take off your clothes and kneel."

I catch a fleeting glimpse of her confusion in the depths of her eyes. Then, with graceful determination, she begins to disrobe, the fabric of her clothing whispering softly as it falls away. Her posture exudes a blend of reverence and quiet strength, as if she's stepping into a role she was always meant to embody.

Her breathtaking beauty captivates my senses and takes my breath away. The soft glow of ambient light embraces her form, casting gentle shadows that contour her every curve. As she lowers to her knees, a cascade of thoughts and emotions tumbles through me, a symphony of admiration, affection, and respect. In this suspended moment, time seems to slow, and the world narrows down to her and me, two souls converging at the crossroads of understanding and desire.

"I've waited for so long to put my collar on you. To show the world you're mine, wholly and without reservation." My voice trembles, revealing the layers of anticipation that have been woven into this moment. "Our journey together has traversed the deepest valleys and scaled the tallest peaks. The road we've walked has been etched with trials that would have shattered lesser bonds. For a time, we waivered, but like a phoenix rising from the ashes, our relationship has emerged with renewed strength. Our relationship, our love, has been tempered by fire, refined by challenge, and burns brighter for all we've endured." I pause and take a deep breath, trying to keep my emotions under control.

"Tonight, I'm offering you my collar not as a simple physical object but as an embodiment of my unwavering dedication to you. It's my promise to be the best Dominant I'm capable of today and to endeavor to be better tomorrow. It's my vow to stand by your side, not just in moments of joy and celebration but also during the trials and tribulations that life may bring. Our love is not confined to the sunniest of days. Rather, it's an anchor that remains steady even in the fiercest storms. With this collar, I pledge to be your rock, shelter, and unyielding support through every chapter of our journey."

I blink away the tears that threaten to escape.

"The promise to respect your boundaries is etched into the very fabric of this commitment. Just as the moon respects the ebb and flow of the tides, I will honor the limits we've set. Yet, hand in hand with this respect, I promise to gently challenge your boundaries, encourage you to explore the realms of your submission, and guide you towards the vistas of personal growth that await. So, with every fiber of my being, every ounce of my heart, I ask you now. Will you permit me to intertwine our fates in an unbreakable bond? Will you consent to wearing my collar?"

"May I say something first, Sir?"

"Yes."

"I'm so undeserving of your collar," she murmurs, her voice tinged with a self-deprecating undertone. I hate hearing her negativity, but in this moment, I choose to let her continue, to allow her voice to weave its thread into the tapestry of vulnerability we're creating. "I know I'm not perfect. I'm acutely aware of my flaws. For most of my life, I've been content with ignoring anything that caused me pain," she reveals, peeling back the layers of her past with candid honesty. "The ache of losing our child and being apart from you were among the most devastating experiences I've endured. Instead of seeking your comfort, I ran and, in doing so, caused us both unspeakable pain. But I've learned an important lesson—a lesson etched in the depths of my being. Regardless of how far I might try to run, I cannot escape the inescapable grip of truth." She looks up at me, and her beautiful blue eyes sparkle.

"As your submissive, I promise to trust you not only with the simple things but, more importantly, with the complexities that reside within the deepest corners of my heart. I recognize that true strength lies in the willingness to share the unfiltered truth, to expose the most fragile facets of my being to you. I do this knowing that everything I tell you will be held with the utmost reverence. With all my heart, I trust that you're strong enough— that we're strong enough to withstand anything life throws at us."

"I vow never to stop learning and growing in my submission. I can't promise to be perfect, but I can promise to work hard to be a better person, a better submissive, than the day before. I'll stand before you as a willing canvas, trusting and open to your guidance and direction. Knowing you'll safeguard my limits while molding me into the submissive I aspire to be." She swipes at the tears streaming down her cheeks in rivulets. "Thank you for allowing me the privilege of being your submissive. I love you, Sir."

Her words humble me, and I kneel before her. "You're everything I could ever imagine in a submissive. Especially on the days you challenge me. It's as if the universe took every hidden desire I've ever had and fashioned you for me." I smile through my tears.

"But, *papillon*, you still didn't answer my question. Will you consent to wearing my collar?"

"I can't think of anything I'd love more. Yes, I consent to wear your collar."

Opening the box, I allow Lana to see it for the first time. Four silver chains extend from a silver ring designed to rest at the base of her throat. Suspended from the ring is a delicate emerald butterfly. "It's exquisite," she breathes, her voice carrying a sense of awe and reverence.

"Green symbolizes growth and new beginnings. You are the butterfly transformation and beauty," I explain, rising from my knees and stepping behind her. As I gently place the collar around her neck, my fingers brush against her skin with the utmost tenderness. "This signifies not only everything you are but everything you've yet to become, *papillon*," I continue, my voice carrying a mixture of conviction and adoration. Securing the collar in place, I extend my hand to her, a silent invitation for her to rise to her feet.

She looks fucking incredible wearing nothing but my ring and collar. My cock is already hard, and we haven't even gotten started.

"Stage one is set for us," I say, waiting for her reaction.

The same St. Andrew's Cross she was restrained to for our first public scene awaits her. My whip rests on the small table beside it, waiting to mark her body.

"I thought we were—"

"Yes, we were going to do a scene in a private room while the club was open. I'm hoping you'll indulge me." She looks at me curiously. "You asked me to be able to have sex with you at the club. I know you meant when there are people here. While I'm unable to fully give you what you've asked for, I want to begin working toward that goal. I've arranged for it to be just you and me tonight. If you let me, I'd love to see you in those cuffs and allow you to feel the caress of the leather against your skin before I fuck you on that stage."

"I would love nothing more, Sir."

She steps up to the cross, keeping her back to me. "Turn around. I have one more gift for you." I pull another set of thin chains from my pocket. "May I?"

"Yes, please."

I attach the top of the chain to the ring of her collar. Her nipples are already hard, but I can't resist bending and taking one into my mouth, sucking and tugging while my fingers play with the other. Releasing it, I take the first clip and tighten the clamp over her nipple, and then I do the same with the other.

I kiss my way down her toned abdomen as I get to my knees. "I've missed tasting you," I say a second before sucking on her clit. Lana lets out a moan. The sound encourages me to continue, and I add my fingers, sliding them in and out while my tongue continues its assault. Her body tenses, and I know she's getting close. With a final nip, I pull away, and she groans. Then, I take the clamp and put it on her swollen clit.

"Turn around," I growl, fighting the urge to skip the scene and fuck her now.

She turns to face the cross, spreading her legs and raising her arms. One by one, I secure her wrists and ankles. I take a few seconds to appreciate the erotic sight before me. Without warning, my hand makes contact with her ass. Over and over, I strike her until her skin is warm and pink.

Tonight, I'm going to test her limits. Svetlana didn't see the small bottle of lube nestled in the coiled leather. Opening it, I squeeze some on my finger. I massage her tight hole before sliding my finger in. She drops her head back with a groan, and I add another finger, stretching her. "Are you ready for more?"

"Mhm," she murmurs softly.

"That isn't consent, papillon," I remind her firmly.

"Yes, Sir. I'm ready for anything you wish to give me," she responds, her voice steady and determined.

When I'm sure she's relaxed and ready, I withdraw my fingers and pick up the silicone toy. After applying a generous amount of lube, I hold it against her. "I'll go slow. Tell me if it's too much." At one time, Lana's body was used to such an invasion, but it's been several years. I don't want to injure her by going too fast.

I begin putting some pressure and pushing the edge of the toy in—her body tenses. "You have to relax," I say, reaching my free hand around her waist and between her legs. With her attention on my fingers in her pussy, her body relaxes, and the toy slides in without further resistance.

I pick up my whip, appreciating the familiar feel of the handle and the way the leather tails soar through the air. After a few practice swings, I turn to face her and pull my arm back, the implement matching my movements until the first lash lands against her skin.

Lana doesn't cry out. Her body relaxes with each strike. I pause, reach into my pocket, and push the button on the tiny remote that controls the butt plug. When it begins vibrating, Lana lets out another seductive moan. My cock is rock hard and begging to sink into her wet heat.

I'm mindful of how long she's had the clamps and know this part of our scene can't last long. Not wanting to waste a second, I allow the whip to make contact over and over in quick succession. The lashes aren't hard, just enough to redden her skin and allow her to forget everything other than what we're doing here.

When I can't take it anymore, I drop my whip and step up behind her. "What's your color?"

"Green, Sir."

Bending down, I undo the restraints around her ankles. Instead of opening the cuffs from her wrists, I release them from the cross, turn her around, and reclip them to the wood.

Lana watches me pull my t-shirt over my head and discard it on the floor. Then I open my jeans, push them and my boxer briefs down my legs, and kick them off to the side. My hard cock is already dripping pre-cum in anticipation of sliding inside her.

I close the distance between us and put my hands under her

thighs. She hooks them around my waist. Her body quivers with need. "This is going to be hard and fast, *papillon*."

The words are barely out of my mouth as I spear my dick inside her and pull the clamp from her clit at the same time. Her body shatters in my arms, squeezing my cock.

"Oh my God, Sir," she says, panting.

I pull out and thrust back inside. It isn't going to take much for me to explode, but I want her to come again. My lips crash against hers as I continue my punishing rhythm. "I missed you so fucking much, Svetlana." I manage to get out between kisses.

"So did I."

"Don't ever leave me again," I warn.

"Never, Sir. I promise."

My hands grasp the remaining clamps. Lana's eyes meet mine just as I tug them off. Her body convulses from the force of her orgasm. I thrust one more time and let go, spilling everything I have into her. After the final waves of pleasure subside, I pull out and carefully set her feet on the floor.

Reaching up, I release her hands. "Are you okay?"

"Yes."

Only when I'm sure she's steady on her feet do I step away to find my jeans to turn the butt plug off.

"Thank you, Brandon. This meant so much to me."

"I know it's not exactly what you asked for, but I promise I'm trying, and one day, we'll do this with a full club."

"I don't care if that ever happens." She cups my cheek. "You don't have to change. I love you exactly the way you are."

Svetlana

I'm collared and engaged to the most wonderful man in the world. Nothing has ever felt more right. Despite everyone hounding us for an answer, we're not setting a date to get married. Eventually, we'll do the whole wedding thing to satisfy everyone who wants to see us say *I do*. But neither of us needs a piece of paper to prove our commitment to one another. As far as we're concerned, the vows we said at Fire and Ice before he collared me are all we need.

The loss of a child and confronting the profound truth that we'll never experience the joy of conceiving a biological child has undoubtedly transformed us, but it hasn't broken us. We know the various alternatives available to us if we should change our minds in the future. Right now, we find ourselves in a place of serene acceptance. Brandon leaves no space for me to question how much he desires me. He leaves no doubt that I'm not any less of a woman because of my inability to conceive a child.

When I stop and look back at my life, I often wish I made better choices and done things differently to spare myself and everyone I love from enduring pain. Yet, in those moments of introspection, Brandon's words resonate with truth. Every decision, regardless of its outcome, has woven the intricate tapestry of my life and has led me to the exact point where destiny intended me to be.

Every day, Brandon embodies the essence of selflessness and unconditional love. In a way that no one else ever could, he's achieved what seemed impossible. He's taught me I don't have to run unless I'm running to him.

He's the quiet to my chaotic mind. The light to my darkness.

We may not have the power to stop life's storms and trials, but as long as we're together, we can withstand anything that dares to cross our path.

Together, we've picked up the pieces of our shattered dreams, taken the lives I believed were fractured, and mended our hearts.

Vmeste na veki.

Some love stories mend what was shattered.

Others begin with two people willing to risk heartbreak anyway.

Continue the Fire & Ice series with Anthony and Leopold in *Love Hurts*.

Or step into a world ruled by obsession, betrayal, and dangerous ambition...

Aoife Quigley is done letting powerful men decide her fate.

Now she's ready to claim the throne they never intended to give her.

Enter the world of *Bound by Darkness*.

Find Tara's Books Here

About Tara

Bestselling author Tara Conrad writes where passion meets peril, crafting dark, spellbinding romances that blur the line between devotion and destruction.

Inspired by the haunting brilliance of Edgar Allan Poe, her stories reimagine Gothic tales with modern sensuality and power.

Within her pages, heroines rise unbroken, villains fall beautifully, and the darkness always tells the truth.

When she isn't writing, Tara travels with her husband, meeting readers who have found pieces of themselves in her worlds.

She believes love isn't always light. Sometimes, it's found in the dark. 🖤

Acknowledgments

George--my Dominant, my husband, my soulmate, my world: this book would not have been possible without Your support and encouragement. Writing about some of the worst times of our lives was not easy, but it was a story that needed to be told, and it was Lana's story that she wanted to share. Thank you for giving me the courage to keep writing, especially on the days I wanted to delete it and pretend it didn't exist. And thank you for being by my side when the doctors told us that each of our babies were no longer with us. Your arms and whispered words of love are the only things that got me through some of those darkest days. I love You.

Dana- I'm humbled you chose to share your story with me. I'd been fighting what I knew Lana's story was supposed to be, but when you told me yours, I knew I had to write it. My heart is bursting watching you start your journey as a mom to a very lucky little girl.

To My Readers- Thank you for taking this journey with Brandon, Lana, and me. It was a rocky road filled with less-than-ideal choices and tragic events, but unfortunately, life isn't always kind. It's about realizing none of us are alone on this crazy adventure. Support is out there—you are NEVER alone.

~Tara

Resources for miscarriage and infertility support: https://resolve.org/get-help/helpline/

https://www.postpartum.net/get-help/loss-grief-in-pregnancy-postpartum/

National Human Trafficking Resource Center 1-888-373-7888

TTY 711

Text HELP to 233733

ONLINE RESOURCES

www.dhs.gov/bluecampaign

polarisproject.org

humantraffickinghotline.org

9 781959 383123